# NEIGHBORHOOD
# BAD
# BLOOD

# NEIGHBORHOOD
# BAD
# BLOOD

## Justin  Fleischman

Published by:
 Editions Dedicaces LLC
   12759 NE Whitaker Way, Suite D833
   Portland, Oregon, 97230
   www.dedicaces.us

Library of Congress Cataloging-in-Publication Data
 Fleischman, Justin.
 Neighborhood Bad Blood / by Justin Fleischman.
 p. cm.

ISBN-13: 978-1-77076-508-5 (alk. paper)
ISBN-10: 1-77076-508-5 (alk. paper)

# Contents

# Part One:
# A Neighborhood Truce

# I.

"Hey, Tyler, how've you been?"
I turned my head and saw Sander Collinworth stepping out of the alleyway across the street as I coasted my bicycle out of my driveway. "I'm okay. What's up?"

"Haven't talked to you in a while."

"I know," I said, wondering why he wanted to speak to me all of the sudden. Our friendship had ended two years earlier when I broke into the Collinworths' house and stole videogames that I really enjoyed playing with Sander and whatever cash I could find. Sander was the one who came home to find me bolting away, and when he reported it, I was arrested. Due to previous offenses —for stealing cigarettes from a local convenience store and running away from home—I spent six months in the Western Pennsylvania Juvenile Correctional Institute, and since being released I'd been homeschooled and had little to no contact with people in my neighborhood.

Sander walked towards me. His brown hair, longer and parted, covered his ears. I recalled his hair buzzed like mine. "We should hang sometime."

"Well, what are you up to now?" I asked looking down, unconvinced Sander was being genuine.

"I don't have any plans. Come on over." Sander turned back towards the alley and waved for me to follow.

I trailed him on my Schwinn ten-speed, slowly pedaling, suspicious and on guard. Through gossip and passing glances, I knew the kids in the neighborhood hated me and would fight me if given the chance. I was worried Sander might be setting me up.

We passed the house where Daryl Leness lived. Sander, Daryl and I were neighbors and our three houses faced Stanberry Hill Road, the major two-lane that sloped down from Chinook Twp. into the city of Briar Mills. Gavy Lane, a street that led up into the residential plan behind us, separated my house from Daryl's. We each lived in corner houses with small side yards opposite each other. Sander lived in the home below Daryl. My driveway opened onto Gavy Lane and directly across, an alley ran behind Daryl's and Sander's. The alley ran even on a ridge behind their houses, so that the backyards slanted up to it.

Shedding my bicycle at the edge of the Collinworths' backyard, I walked with Sander to a clearing where burnt sticks laid in the pit and more wood was stacked three feet high at the edge of his yard. Beyond that, trees stretched downward to Stanberry Hill Road. The yard looked different than I recalled from when we used to play football here.

"We sometimes have a bonfire here, probably going to have one Friday night. Want to come?" asked Sander.

I remained silent and cautious, wondering why Sander was being so friendly.

He looked at me and smiled. "It's cool if you come, dude."

"Sure." I paused. "How's Daryl been?" I asked, knowing he would be attending the bonfire.

"Daryl? Oh, that guy's way too damn much sometimes."

"How so?" I never knew Daryl that well. He was mostly Sander's friend. But I knew he had a troublesome home life. Once I saw him running out of his house and falling down the front porch steps. His father came out and chased him up Gavy Lane, tripped and landed on his face, then got up and started cursing at Daryl. Daryl trembled looking down at him. His father eventually moved out and I never found out why he left or where he moved to.

Sander lightly chuckled and shook his head. "You remember Fenton?"

"Of course I do."

He heaved a sigh. "The three of us were at the Kinosha Valley Mall a while ago and me and Fenton were in the Best Buy across from Macy's. We thought Daryl was still in Macy's. But when we came out of Best Buy, Daryl was out of the parking lot, sitting on a guardrail, staring at the cars. We started walking towards him and he motioned for us to stay away."

"Uh huh," I said, bobbing my head, staring at him.

"So Fenton and me just chilled at Best Buy, wondering what that crazy asshole was doing. And after about ten minutes we heard a lady scream and I turned to find this lady running through the parking lot carrying a crying baby."

My eyes widened. "What?"

"Daryl started laughing and we ran to him, knowing he did something." He shook his head. "He wouldn't tell us right away, but as we left the mall parking lot, Daryl told us just before he left Macy's he took a baby from a stroller, took it out into the parking lot, found an unlocked car and placed the baby on the seat."

"What? Are you putting me on?"

Sander shook his head. "I know! I couldn't believe it myself. Who does shit like that? But Daryl got a big kick out of it. He was laughing on the way home, saying 'That'll teach that mother to keep an eye on her kid.'"

I was going to ask why he associated with a guy like that, but thought if I did, he might've brought up when I broke into his house and other foolish crimes I'd committed, even though none were that drastic. "When was this?"

"Few weeks before school let out."

"Was the baby okay?"

He nodded. "We could hear it screaming and crying as the lady ran through the parking lot and back into the mall." He paused. "So I can only take Daryl in small doses anymore. If he wants to hang out here at the bonfires, that's okay. But I won't be going back to the mall with him again, at least not anytime soon."

I shook my head. If he was telling the truth, it seemed Daryl had made a change for the worse, at least since the time that I knew him.

We spent almost an hour talking about times when we were friends, playing football in the yard, basketball at the playground and venturing through the woods, avoiding anything about our feud and my paranoia lessened. Then, Sander led me through the yard and into the basement. Rhododendrons lined the cracked sidewalk and we entered through the basement door, walking into a finished-off basement with purple carpeting, a pool table, couch, chair and a large, widescreen television. "Nice," I said.

"Thanks. We spend a lot of time here."

I wondered who 'we' were.

"During football season, a bunch of us come here to watch the games," said Sander, turning on the TV.

Sitting on the sofa, watching the television, I believed he was speaking of friends and family and I wondered how they would feel if they knew Sander let me into the house I was banished from and that he invited me to a gathering of theirs.

# 2.

F riday evening came and I was hesitant to cross the street and go to the bonfire, believing it possible Sander's invitation was so he could attack me with friends. Thinking it would be smart to bring a weapon of some sort I hid a pocketknife in my shorts pocket and went over.

Entering the yard, I saw flames burning in the pit.

Sander turned hearing me coming. "Tyler, glad you could make it."

"Thanks," I said. The basement door opened and Mr. Collinworth came out, smiling, and I was unsure of what to expect.

"Tyler Dyson! It's been a while," nodded Mr. Collinworth.

"Mr. Collinworth, nice to see you," I said as friendly as I could, thinking the man had become grayer.

As Sander and his father talked by the fire, Daryl walked over from his house with Fenton Lay. I trembled slightly as they stared.

"Tyler!" Daryl grinned. "What's up?"

I bit my upper lip. "Sander invited me over," I said, almost defensively. Daryl had slicked back blonde hair and his chest was broad. I remembered him being skinnier.

"Yeah, he's cool," said Sander, glancing past his father.

Daryl walked by me as Fenton approached. His skin tone was dark and his black hair was long and straight, much longer than I remembered.

"Hey, Tyler." Fenton stuck out his hand and I shook it, remembering how the last time we spoke I made fun of him for having a white mother and Asian father.

Mr. Collinworth left and we sat by the fire. Fenton took out a pack of cigarettes and handed Daryl one then lit them.

As darkness settled and the full moon shined, we cooked hot dogs and drank sodas—which was just fine with me. Then Daryl talked about getting beer and weed and it reminded me of my how past recklessness and had pushed the three of them away. But I didn't mention it.

Daryl disappeared for a while then returned with two six-packs of Budweiser.

"Where's the reefer?" asked Fenton.

"That was a little harder to get. Maybe next time."

Sitting by the fire, Daryl surprisingly offered me a beer and I declined.

"Come on, Tyler," laughed Fenton. "You were smoking and drinking before any of us with those assholes Rick and Jester."

I turned away, hearing Daryl's squealing laugh that always used to annoy me. I couldn't believe Fenton had brought up Rick and Jester, two guys from the past I would much rather have forgotten about.

"Leave him alone, Fenton," Sander sharply said, placing another log into the fire.

Later on, we left the dying fire to go into the basement. Daryl and Fenton staggered inside after Sander and me. Fenton stuck his hand out to me and flung back his hair. "Sorry 'bout what I said."

"That's okay." I shook his hand, truly wanting to forget about it.

Daryl racked balls on the pool table. "Anybody up for a game?"

Hunched over, Fenton staggered to the couch and fell on it, hard, then slowly rolled off.

"These guys didn't have that much to drink," Sander said. "They're just being jackasses."

I laughed, sitting on the couch as Sander turned on the television.

Fenton got up and shot pool with Daryl, taking several breaks to go outside and smoke. After the third game, they were ready to leave. "Hey Sander, thanks for having us," said Daryl. "The beer's all gone, so we're taking off."

"Yeah, we'll probably be doing it again in a couple of days," said Sander.

"I'll have some dope then," laughed Daryl. Sander shook his head.

"Hey, Tyler, don't take anything that isn't yours!" Fenton yelled.

I stared, astounded as they left.

"I'm sorry about that, Tyler," Sander said sincerely.

I bowed my head and sighed. "Maybe I still don't fit in here."

"You're cool with me now, and you're cool with them," Sander said in a reassuring tone. "They just say dumb shit."

I didn't mention anything more about it and shortly after midnight, I left. Walking the short distance home, I removed the knife I'd forgotten about from my pocket and laughed, believing Sander was starting to become a friend again.

# 3.

Waking the next day at 11:00, I found my mother in the kitchen cleaning.

"Hey Tyler, what time did you get in last night?"

"Don't remember," I said, removing an orange juice bottle from the refrigerator.

"Were you at the Collinworths' the whole time?"

"Yeah, Sander had a bonfire."

She stared at me, smiling. "I'm glad there's no more bad blood between you two."

I'd never mentioned Sander to her since returning home from juvie. She, like me, probably thought we'd never get along again. "We're cool now."

"It's good you're friends again."

"Yeah," I nodded, "I'm happy about it too."

After having brunch I sat on the couch and turned on the television and recalled how I rarely rode my bicycle down or around Gavy Lane, feeling no good could come from that. In the year-and-a half that I'd been home, I would sometimes see the guys and immediately turn away. It was hard to avoid them completely and my bicycle was my transport out of the neighborhood.

Plus, everybody around knew my reputation and I received my share of angry and dubious glances. My relationship with Daryl, Fenton and Mr. Collinworth still seemed problematic, and I assumed it still was with most people in the neighborhood. My mother once told me that, in time, people would forget. I didn't know if that was true.

———— ⚭ ————

Two days later the phone rang and the ID read, "Collinworth."

"Hello."

"Is Tyler there?" asked Sander.

"Right here, Sander. What's up?"

"Hey, Tyler, we're having another fire tonight if you want to come."

"Yeah, why wouldn't I come?" I asked but then felt I shouldn't have.

"I'll get it started around seven. There'll be some different people here."

"Daryl and Fenton aren't coming?" I thought it might be better if they didn't show.

"Yeah, man. As far as I know, they'll be here. But my girlfriend's going to stop by."

"Do I know her?"

"I don't know. Tamara Nicholas ring a bell?"

I vaguely remembered her from school. She had curly, black hair and was a little chunky. I didn't remember talking to her much, and being that I was going to see her, felt relieved. Back in the local school, there were girls I would harass. "Yeah, I remember her."

"Cool," Sander said.

"Do you need any help setting up?"

"Uh, my dad's going to help out when he gets home from work. But you can stop by early if you want."

"Yeah, maybe I will," I said, but doubted it, due to the discomforting impression I had felt from Mr. Collinworth.

"Okay, yeah, whatever," said Sander.

After hanging up, I worried about heading over. If there was going to be drinking, someone might refer to my past again. But if I didn't attend, that might not look good, especially after already accepting Sander's invitation.

# 4.

Wearing khaki shorts, I slid on thong sandals and stepped outside, feeling tenser than the other night. I worried Daryl or Fenton could embarrass me again.

The fire burned slightly as I came into the yard. Sander sat roasting two hotdogs.

"Sup, Tyler?" Sander said, his face masked with perspiration and sweat dripping from his hair.

"You and your dad got everything done?"

"Yeah, we finished chopping wood and setting up about ten minutes ago."

I didn't see Mr. Collinworth and wondered where he was.

The basement door opened and Tamara walked out texting on her cell.

"Tamara, come here!" Sander waved her over.

Her hair was still curly but she was not as chubby as I recalled. Her tight pink shirt could be seen through slightly to her black bra and she didn't look bad now.

"Tamara, this is my good friend, Tyler Dyson."

She placed her phone in her back pocket and shook my hand. "Yeah, I remember Tyler." She smiled. "You used to go to school with us."

"Yeah." I glanced away.

"Where do you go to school now?" It was the question I knew was coming.

"I don't go anywhere. It's summer," I answered with a smile.

Sander laughed. "Hey babe could you go get us two cans of Pepsi, please?"

I thought he was trying to change the subject.

"I can't lift that big cooler," she said. "I mean, with all the pop and ice in it."

"Not asking you to bring the cooler, just two cans."

"That's all right, Sander. I don't need one now," I said.

"Well, I need a pop fix." He removed the hot dogs from the fire. "Don't nobody eat my dog. I'll be right back." He put the stick on the ground, placing the hot dog back into the fire and went towards the house.

"Sander, grab me one too!" I yelled. Sander waved back.

"So, you and Sander have been friends for a long time?" asked Tamara.

"Actually," I paused, carefully choosing my words, "we sort of drifted apart over the last couple of years. I'm homeschooled now and, well, we just didn't see much of each other."

"I remember you from when you went to school with us."

I wasn't sure if she remembered or even knew the trouble I got into. If she did recall, I was glad she wasn't bringing it up.

"So, where do you live?" she asked.

"Not far. Just right across the street."

"And I've never seen you around before?"

Sander returned with two cans of Pepsi and Tamara asked nothing more. I knew she was left confused.

Not too much later, Fenton arrived. "Hey, Fenton," I said casually as he walked by.

"Hey," Fenton said, not looking at me.

As dusk settled, Daryl came over with two friends, Chris and Ron, and we all sat around the fire laughing and joking. Tamara was the only female there. I noticed the guys taking a peek at her and wondered if Sander saw or even minded that they did.

"Tyler," said Chris. "Fenton was telling us you haven't been hanging around here the last couple of years."

I turned to Fenton. His expression was plain. "Um, no, I guess not."

"Why not? What's wrong, man? Isn't this your neighborhood?"

I turned away, angry over Fenton brining that up and wondered what else he could've told them.

"Leave him alone, Chris!" Fenton hollered. He smiled, stood and came towards me. "He got into a little trouble when he was younger, but he's cool now." He applied a light headlock and rubbed my head.

Although the embrace was cordial, I looked away and sighed, not approving of Fenton bringing up what happened back then.

Chris put a cigarette in his mouth and lit it.

"Chris, don't smoke now. My dad might come out," said Sander.

"It's only a cigarette, not a joint." He removed it from his lips.

"Just chill out for a little while—until it gets darker."

"Already lit, Sander." He put it back into his mouth and slowly said, "I'm not putting it out. I gots to smoke it."

A little later, as it became darker, Daryl said something to Sander as he placed a log into the fire. Sander nodded and Daryl walked away. Between that and questions about my relationships with the Collinworths and everybody else in the neighborhood, it generated an uncomfortable environment. "Excuse me a second," I said to Fenton and Ron getting up and going to Sander.

"Hey Tyler," Sander said, as I approached.

"Where'd Daryl go?"

"These guys want to drink, so he went to get some beers."

"Oh," I said, standing next to Sander, staring at the flames. Knowing everybody would be drinking when Daryl returned, and possibly smoking weed, I thought maybe it would be best to leave. I wouldn't be drinking and didn't want to be a prude to everyone else. Ever since being released from juvenile detention, I'd avoided drinking and drugs, and really never had a problem doing it. Although that wasn't the main reason I was sent away, there were some experiences with it. Once in juvie, I saw someone with dilated pupils, chills and shakes due to heroin withdrawal and that made me want to avoid all illegal drugs. Turning away from Sander, I stared into the darkness.

"Tyler."

I turned to him.

"Hey, listen, I can tell you're not into drinking. That's fine, dude. I don't think I'm going to drink much tonight."

We walked away from the fire together and I wondered what Sander's definition of 'much' was.

Sander went back to sit by Tamara. I assumed he wanted to be alone with his girl and I went over to the guys.

Daryl came back with a cooler, wearing a light jacket. Setting the cooler down, he opened it, revealing many cans of Miller High Life in ice. Daryl, Fenton, Chris and Ron each grabbed a can. "Hey, Sander, want one?" asked Daryl.

"A little later," Sander said, still sitting with Tamara.

"Yeah, yeah, it's all right." Daryl strutted back, bobbing his head. Reaching inside his jacket, he pulled out a small bag with two joints. He lit one, took a hit and passed it to Fenton.

I turned away and walked towards Sander and Tamara.

"Tyler," Sander said smiling. "What's up?"

"Well, them guys got pot," I looked at the ground grinning. "And, well, I really don't want to be around it."

Sander nodded and looked down. That wasn't the response I was expecting. I turned away and stared into the darkness, then looked down while Sander and Tamara whispered back and forth to one another.

The two stood and went towards the others. I hesitated, and then after Sander said something to Daryl and he laughed, I slowly walked over. Daryl gave the joint to Sander and, surprisingly to me, he took a hit. I didn't know why it startled me. I was just starting to become friends with Sander again and I didn't know him very well yet.

When the smell of burning marijuana hit me, it brought back memories of the few experiences I'd had. Rick and Jester would often smoke in Rick's basement and act rambunctious. Rick once knocked over a lamp, shattering it and we all thought that was hilarious. For the first time since I'd been home and out of juvie, I began to feel slightly tempted to smoke.

Ron took a hit and attempted to pass it to me and I just walked away, without saying a word, and removed a Pepsi from the cooler. I expected Ron to ask why I didn't want a hit but was relieved he didn't.

Tamara grabbed a beer and leaned against Sander, holding his hand. Daryl and Chris finished smoking the roach as everyone except me drank around the fire.

"I'll be right back," said Ron, standing.

"Where're you going?" asked Sander.

"I got a little CD player in my car. I'm going to play some music. It's too quiet out here."

"Yeah, just don't blast it too loud. Might piss the neighbors off," said Sander.

Chris took out his cigarettes. "Man, I still feel like smoking." He stuck one in his mouth and lit it.

I stared at him, wanting a cigarette.

"Hey, what's your name, again?" Chris asked, noticing my gaze.

"That's Tyler," Sander said.

"Tyler, you want a cigarette?"

"Uh, no thanks."

Ron returned with the radio, playing Jay-Z.

"Shit," Daryl said, shaking his head.

"What's wrong?" I asked.

"I hate this rap shit," said Daryl. "It's a good thing I'm a little stoned, or else I'd—"

"You'd what?" asked Ron, leaning back, sipping his brew.

"I'd probably smash your damn radio."

Sander and I both laughed.

"Got a problem with black people?" asked Ron.

"What?" Daryl yelled. "I didn't say that! All I said was I hate rap. That shit sucks! I need to hear some guitar with my music!"

"Okay, Daryl," said Sander. "You don't have to get loud about it."

"Shit." Daryl shook. "I don't hate anybody." He looked at Fenton. "One of my best friends is. . ." he paused, "is an Oriental."

"Fuck you!" Fenton blurted.

I snickered.

"Fuck you too, Tyler!"

"Chill out!" ordered Sander. "I don't know. Maybe the pot's making you guys a little hostile."

I grinded my teeth, trembled slightly and looked down, wondering why Fenton swore at me and believing Sander accused me of hitting the joint. But I stayed silent. The night progressed and everyone talked and laughed and subjects changed frequently.

"Ron, what time is it?" asked Chris.

Ron looked at his phone. "A little after eleven."

"Okay," Chris said, "we'll hang out, sober up for about a half-hour, then we gots to go!"

"I don't know how I'm getting home," said Tamara.

"We can drop you off," offered Chris.

"You wouldn't mind?" she asked.

"She doesn't live too far out of the way, Chris," said Sander.

"Yeah, no problem."

"Thanks, Chris," smiled Sander. "Her parents might get mad if she stays here the entire night. I don't think they trust me."

Everybody but Tamara laughed.

After Chris, Ron and Tamara departed, the rest of us went into the basement.

"I'm going to head home now," I said, feeling a little famished.

"You're leaving?" Daryl asked.

"No, no Tyler," said Sander, "hang out a little while."

"Yeah, Tyler, stick around," smiled Daryl.

"Okay, I'll stay for a little bit." I sat on the couch.

"Anybody up for a game?" asked Fenton, racking balls on the pool table.

Daryl slowly went over and grabbed a pool stick. "I'll break."

Sander turned on the television and sat beside me.

"The carnival's next week," Daryl said, shooting the cue ball, breaking the rack.

"Yeah!" nodded Sander.

"Do you guys want to check it out?" asked Daryl.

There was silence, until Fenton said: "He likes them carnival fries. Looks forward to eating 'em all year."

Daryl snickered. "That's true, that's true."

"You want to check it out next week?" Sander asked me.

"Sure," I responded, "I don't think I went to it last year. I'll go with you guys."

"All right, sounds good," Daryl said.

I listened for a response from Fenton but heard nothing. I thought Fenton might've made a discouraging remark about me coming.

Sander changed channels on the television and noticed The Sixth Sense starting.

"Cool," he said.

"What?" I asked.

"The Sixth Sense is on."

"Oh, man, that movie's too freaky," said Fenton, chalking his pool stick.

"Yeah, slant-eye here is used to movies about dinosaurs destroying Tokyo. Those movies ain't freaky at all," said Daryl.

Fenton fake laughed.

Sander and I sat on the couch in the dark watching the movie. The only light came from the TV and the ceiling lamp above the pool table.

After shooting two games, Daryl and Fenton left as Sander and I continued to watch TV and a little later, we both drifted to sleep.

# 5.

I awoke, disoriented, unsure of where I was. "Oh shit." I remembered falling asleep at Sander's. "Shit, shit." I stood. "What the hell time is it?"

Sander slightly awoke. "What the hell?"

"Sander, you fell asleep. We fell asleep watching that stupid movie." Turning on the light, I looked at the clock. "Damn, it's 5:30."

"Okay, shut the light off," said Sander, stretching out on the couch.

After hitting the switch, I exited, angered over Sander's falling asleep.

Stepping in the front door of my house, all was dark and quiet as I crept up the stairs, passing my parents' bedroom and entering my own. Quickly removing my clothes and plopping into bed, I thought I may have gotten away with staying out all night and drifted to sleep.

Not much later, a hand roughly shook my shoulder. Looking up, Dad stood there. He wore glasses with brown frames and his black goatee, that needed trimmed, stood out. He was not in his work clothes and I knew he must've just woken up.

"Hey, Dad." I opened my eyes slightly. "What's up?"

"What time did you get in?"

"Don't remember," I answered, closing my eyes completely.

"Hey, get up!" Dad yelled.

"Yeah," I sighed, exasperated.

"I was talking to you. Don't think you can blow me off! What were you doing all night?"

"I was just over Sander's."

"All night?"

"What?" I questioned, but knew what he said.

"I know you were over there all night!" he hollered. "I woke up at two, came to see if you were home, and you weren't!"

"Well," I yawned, "we went inside to watch a movie and fell asleep."

Dad sighed and turned away. "Don't sleep in too much today. I want you to cut the grass. And it's going to get humid later on. It would be best if you did it sooner rather than later." He then noticed clothes on the floor. "And put your clothes away." Picking them up, he took a whiff. "Better yet, put them in the hamper. Was there a fire? These smell like smoke and need washed."

"What?" I rolled to the side.

"Your clothes smell like smoke. Did Sander have a fire?"

I sighed. "Yeah, Dad, I told you Sander was having a bonfire."

"Right," he paused. "I forgot there was a bonfire. I'll put these in the hamper. Don't forget to cut the grass."

"What's going on, Phil?" I heard Mom ask.

"He stayed out all night and now wants to sleep all day!"

I sat up, and threw the pillow at the door, then rolled over, angry with my father. Those guys were smoking and drinking and I got lectured just because I fell asleep at Sander's.

I was unable to fall back asleep.

After my parents left for their jobs—Mom, an RN at the Chinook Medical Center and Dad, an auto-repair man at Westley's Garage—I got up and headed downstairs. Looking at a picture of me and my elder sister, Teresa, in the hall, I knew my parents never had half the trouble with her as they did with me. She'd been married a little over a year and moved from our western Pennsylvania town to South Bend, Indiana. Before she moved, I never realized how much I'd miss her. Just as I used to argue with my parents, there were quarrels with her also. Once, the screaming got so intense that I grabbed her hair, pulled her to the ground and almost punched her, but Dad stopped me. The incident was never discussed. But I'd thought about it often and still felt rotten over it.

Although I would never do anything like that again, a slight part of me wanted to get drunk and smoke cigarettes. That would've really made my parents angry. But I knew that would be in nobody's best interest. Leaning back in the recliner, I turned on the television and after a few minutes, dozed off.

Upon waking a couple hours later, I shut the television off and went into the kitchen, to eat a quick breakfast before beginning the yard work.

# 6.

I started the lawnmower in the back yard, thinking I probably should've just left Sander's with Fenton and Daryl did. If I would've done that, Dad wouldn't have given me such a hard time this morning and I might've started mowing the lawn sooner.

After finishing the front, I proceeded to the back and noticed Sander approaching. Stopping, I wiped my forehead.

"Sup?"

I nodded. "Just cutting the lawn."

"Hey, I'm sorry I fell asleep. I remember hearing you yell waking up." He bit his tongue, I could tell, to keep from laughing.

"Oh, dude, that's okay. I got a little lecture from my dad this morning. He didn't want me staying out all night."

"What time did you wake up and leave?"

"I think it was almost six."

"Oh, man."

"Yeah, you know the way parents think: 'nothing good can be happening when the kids are out all night.'"

Sander just bowed his head.

"Yeah, but it's no big deal." I said, wishing I could retract my last statement.

"Cool. I won't hold you up while you're cutting the grass. I was just wondering what time you left."

As he walked away, I didn't want him to leave. "Sander!"

He turned.

"Hey, I'll be done working soon. You want to do something? I mean, if you don't have other plans."

"Yeah, that's cool. I'll be at home. Just stop over when you're done."

After finishing the lawn, I showered and shaved, then put the grungy clothes back on. Heading to the Collinworths' house, I pondered what we could do. When we were younger, we used to like going into the woods. But I didn't know if Sander would be up for that. I thought he might be interested in going to the playground to shoot hoops.

Going through the backyard, I went to the basement door, figuring that's where Sander would be. After three knocks, with no answer, I moved away and Sander opened the door. He was dressed in khaki shorts and a red polo shirt. I knew any plans I thought about were shot.

"Sorry, I was upstairs," he said.

"Yeah."

"I got to go out with Tamara in about a half hour. Sorry, maybe we can do something later."

"Sure."

"Okay, I'll stop over when I get back."

I just nodded.

"See you later, buddy."

Turning away as the door closed, I walked home cursing and shaking my head, wondering why he couldn't have just told me he had plans with Tamara.

Passing Daryl's house, I thought about stopping, but then felt my relationship with him wasn't strong enough to just drop by. Plus, hanging out with Daryl alone was something I didn't think I wanted to do. So when I got home, I took out my bicycle and rode it across the main street, out of the neighborhood.

———————

Sitting with my parents that evening and watching TV, I didn't hear from Sander. Part of me wanted to walk over and see what he was doing. But I already went there once today and was turned away for the girlfriend, so I wasn't going over again.

Then I wondered about the future with the neighborhood clique. It seemed the hatchet was buried with Sander. We at least were talking and getting along. With the other guys, my association still seemed questionable.

# 7.

That Monday morning, Sander called.
"Hey Tyler, it's Sander."

"Hey, what's up?"

"Got any plans for tonight? Or any night this week?"

"Not for tonight." I wondered what he was getting at.

"Cool, you know the carnival's back in town. We're all going to check it out. Planning on going every night."

"Every night?"

"Well, like I said, that's the plan. You know, sometimes I see people from school there I haven't seen all summer. Different kids come on different nights and, well, we like seeing who shows up."

It didn't seem impossible to go every night. It was being held near the elementary school, which was only about a mile away. "I'll go tonight."

"Yeah, and who knows? Maybe, if we're up for it, have another bonfire afterwards?"

"Sounds good."

"All right—"

"Sander!"

"Yeah?"

I wanted to mention I didn't feel comfortable around the pot and beer at the fires. But, with being on the phone and not knowing if his parents were around, decided not to. "Nothing, I'll talk to you later."

"Okay, dude, we'll all be in the backyard ready to leave at, oh, about six."

"I'll be over."

"Cool."

"One more thing, Sander, who's 'we?'"

"You know, you, me, Daryl and Fenton."

"Yeah, right. I was wondering if Tamara was going"

"Okay, dude, I'll be at home. Stop over anytime." He hung up the phone.

---

I walked over at 5:40 and found Sander, Daryl and Fenton stacking timber near the flameless pit. Sander turned, hearing me coming. "Okay, Tyler's here."

"Yeah, everybody quit talking about his sister!" Fenton laughed.

I pretended I didn't hear that.

"Want to head over now?" Sander asked, removing his work gloves.

"Were you guys waiting for me?" I asked.

"No, not really," answered Fenton. "We were just chilling and thought it'd be a good idea to get wood ready for the next fire."

"We ain't in no hurry," Daryl said. "My mom said I could use her car tonight. I don't know if she knows it, but I'm going to use her car every night this week." He laughed. "Going to be using it for whatever the hell I want."

I got in the back of the Nissan with Sander and Fenton rode shotgun. Pulling out of the driveway and up Stanberry Hill Road, we made a left on Quarles Road. Daryl put a cigarette in his mouth.

"Want me to light that for you?" Fenton asked.

"Not now, man," Daryl said. "I'm just getting it ready for after we park. I don't want to smoke in the car. 'Cause then I'd have to hear my mom bitch."

"Does she know you smoke?" I asked.

He shrugged his shoulders.

We pulled into a church parking lot, which was three blocks away from the school. Exiting the car, Daryl lit his cigarette.

Moving along in the humidity, we made a right up a back street passing three houses and came to another road, half closed-off for vendors. Several stands had activities to win prizes in the semi-crowded area. Small rides, along with a couple large ones, surrounded us. We walked along the dead grass to a township building, where food was being sold. The fresh smell of hamburgers, hotdogs and french-fries filled the area.

"We're getting food right away?" I asked, following them to get in line.

"Yeah," said Sander. "Do you remember what Fenton said about Daryl and carnival fries?"

"I remember."

We each purchased a small order of french-fries and a Coke and sat on benches to eat.

"Daryl, you going to get another order of fries when you're done?" asked Sander.

"Not right away."

"Yeah, but you'll be back there before the night is through," laughed Fenton.

I started to really have a good time and was looking forward to the rest of the evening, in a way I hadn't been excited in a while.

Finishing our food, we each purchased a "Ride All Evening" stamp then found the largest, most frightful ride there. It was gold and over thirty-feet high. Several oval carts were attached that could fit two persons inside. The large wheel spun around and went upside down, circling rapidly and was called the "Super-Spinner." I entered a chamber with Sander, and Fenton and Daryl climbed into one behind us. It started out slowly, picking up speed. We laughed as we were jostled roughly about. Getting off the ride, we were still laughing, feeling dizzy.

Daryl and Fenton were soon drawn away and Sander and I rode the Ferris wheel. "I don't know what they're doing," said Sander, "but if we paid eight bucks for the riding stamp, I'm not going to waste the money."

"Right."

"Well, you know, they are a bit older than us, so maybe they got other plans." He paused. "Whatever, who cares."

I laughed.

Strolling along, we found Tamara with two of her friends.

"Sander!" she yelled, running over and hugging him.

"Relax, babe," Sander smiled, returning the embrace.

"This is my boyfriend, Sander," she said to the girls. "Sander, this is Ashton, and you know Melisssa."

I examined Ashton's slim body and long straight brown hair as she shook Sander's hand. Turning away, I intentionally coughed.

Sander turned to me. "Tamara, aren't you going to introduce Tyler?"

"I'm sorry, Tyler. This is Ashton and Melissa."

I shook hands with both of them. "Yeah, I think I know Melissa," I said, nonchalantly. "Ashton, I've never met."

Ashton laughed. "I don't really live around here. I'm just here for the summer, visiting my dad."

"That explains why I've never met you," smiled Sander.

"No," she shook her head, "I don't go to school with you all."

Sensing an opportunity, I got in on the conversation. "Yeah, Ashton, I don't go to school with them either."

"Don't you live around here?"

"I live near Sander."

"Tyler's homeschooled," Sander said, putting his arm around Tamara.

"You are?" Ashton questioned. "Why? I mean, how does that work?"

I figured it'd be best to give a short answer. "It gets lonely."

"Yeah, I'm sure it would. I assume you're taught all by yourself. There're no other kids involved, right?"

"Just me," I answered.

"Tamara, what do you say we find some rides to go on," Sander said with a wink, and putting his other arm around Melissa, he turned and walked away with them.

I knew, with the wink and taking the other girls away, he was leaving me alone with Ashton and I didn't mind.

"So, do you want to walk?" she asked.

I strolled forward and she followed.

"This is like, the first night I've actually been out since I got here."

"How long've you been here?"

"Oh, about a month. I know how you feel, I mean, with feeling lonely."

"So. . .your summer's been kind of, uneventful?"

"Yeah," she paused. "Well, Tamara's been a good friend—actually, my only friend here."

I understood the concept of not having many friends, or at least thought I did.

"Sometimes she likes to go off with her other friends, or Sander. I understand. It's no big deal."

I continued listening.

"Back home, I mean, living with my mom, I have a bunch of friends. Not so much here."

I asked questions about living with her mother as we walked and the evening progressed and eventually learned her last name was Jensen. I really enjoyed having a girl to talk to, but tried not to appear as happy as I was. After purchasing sodas, we sat on a bench.

"So you and Sander are good friends?" she asked, finally not speaking of herself.

I thought it had been a while since anyone had dared to ask that. I used to get angry just hearing his name. "Sure."

"I don't know him that well, but he seems nice."

I didn't know him much better than her anymore, but said nothing.

As the sun eventually set, we continued to talk, most of it done by Ashton. I saw Daryl and Fenton go by with some friends, and Sander walked by with Tamara and winked at me. Lowering my head, I smiled and heard Ashton giggle.

Ashton chatted away as we walked along and I just listened to her.

Her eyes suddenly opened wide with surprise. "Cool, a carousel!" She squealed in delight over the colorfully painted horses.

I followed her to get in line behind four young kids.

"When I was a little girl, I loved coming to the fair and riding with my dad on the horses." She paused. "It just reminds me of when I was little, going out with my mom and my dad, days that'll never happen again."

As we got on separate plastic horses, I wondered if she talked like this to everyone. She seemed like a nice, polite girl—maybe too tactful for me and the guys. The music started and the horses went around, going up and down. I could tell that she very much enjoyed moving slowly on the ponies.

When the ride was over, we continued walking and Ashton lightly body-checked me. I looked down, smiling, not wanting this time to end.

"So what do you and Tamara's boyfriend do for fun."

"Well, to tell you the truth, Ashton, we just started hanging out again recently."

"You did?"

"Yeah, we mostly just chill in his backyard. I guess we don't hang out that much. He's usually busy with Tamara."

She giggled then said, "Tyler, do you want to go down the slide with me?"

"Sure."

I followed her to the twenty-foot high Fun Slide, which had two individual slides and got in line behind two small kids. After the kids went, screaming the entire way down, we sat on green pads and went down, going over two bumps along the way. Ashton laughed loudly when we reached the bottom.

After that, we came to a basketball-shooting stand. I picked up a small basketball.

"Want to give it a try?" the carnie asked.

I noticed stuffed animals along the sidewall. "What do I got to do win a prize?"

"Five bucks gets you three shots. You make all three, you win a prize. And I'll give you a free practice shot."

"Want a stuffed bear?" I asked Aston.

"I like the stuffed lion," she replied.

"First shot's a free practice shot," the man repeated.

"Okay." I handed the man five dollars and shot, making the basket.

"Three more," he said.

I made another basket, missed one and made the last one.

"Okay, thank you," he said, turning away.

"Do I get a stuffed animal?"

"Nope."

"Why not? I made three shots."

"That first shot was a practice. If you missed that one and made the rest, you'd get a prize."

"That's okay, Tyler," Ashton said. "Let's go for a walk."

I turned away. "I should've got a prize. I made three shoots."

"Well, these people are just like everybody else—out to make a buck."

I smiled, pretending I wasn't upset over blowing five dollars.

"Come on," Ashton said. "I'll buy you a Coke."

She purchased the beverages and stood next to me near the edge of the concession stand.

"I had fun tonight, Ashton."

She nodded, sipping her drink.

"How much longer are you going to be around? I mean, before you go back to your mom's?"

"Oh, another few weeks."

I wanted to tell her I'd like to see her again, but didn't want to appear eager. "Are you coming back with Tamara?"

"Back where with Tamara?"

I laughed. "Back here at the carnival."

"Are you going to be back here at the carnival?"

"Yeah, Sander and me were talking about coming every night."

"Well, then you'll see me. I'll be back here. Maybe even tomorrow."

Tamara and Melissa approached us with Melissa talking on her cell.

"Ashton, Melissa's Mom's waiting for us. Time to go," said Tamara.

Ashton turned to me. "Okay, Tyler, I have to leave."

"I'll see you."

She followed the girls and waved back at me. Watching her leave, I hoped we'd have a chance to talk again.

Sander suddenly appeared with Daryl and Fenton. "Hey, Tyler, you ready to take off?"

"Yeah, man, whenever," I answered, knowing the best part of the evening was over. I again glanced in the direction Ashton went, but couldn't find her. I looked at Sander. "You know anything about that girl?"

"Dude, I just met her tonight."

Daryl and Fenton started heading off, and Sander and I followed. I felt down about how quickly the evening ended. I couldn't stop thinking about Ashton and wanted to see her again.

"So who's the honey you were drooling over all night?" Fenton asked.

"Her name's Ashton, real nice girl."

"Get any?" Daryl asked.

"I wasn't drooling," I said, ignoring Daryl.

"No, but you had your arrow pointing, showing her which way to go," said Daryl. They all laughed.

I was getting used to their sense of humor but then wondered if the girls had dragged her away because of something the guys said. I tried to convince myself they wouldn't do that to me.

The clock read 10:20 as we pulled into Daryl's driveway. I didn't have to be home until midnight. I didn't want to go home and didn't feel like hanging out with the guys either. All I thought about was Ashton and when I'd see her again.

"Sander, you feel like starting a fire?" Daryl asked.

"I ain't tired."

"Is that a yes?" asked Fenton.

"Sure." Sander exited the car.

Sander, Fenton and I went to the pit and each placed a log inside. Sander ripped newspaper, lit it and threw it in then squirted gas.

"Where'd Daryl go?" I asked, realizing he wasn't around.

"He'll be back," said Fenton.

He returned minutes later, smoking a cigarette and carting two six-packs of Miller High Life. Sander and Fenton each grabbed a can. Of course, I didn't care to.

Sitting around the fire, they spoke of sports. First about baseball, then what our favorite football teams, the Pittsburgh Steelers and Dallas Cowboys might do this year.

I didn't say much. I was thinking of Ashton and when I'd see her again. "Hey guys, think I'm going to head home now," I said, standing

"Getting bored?" asked Daryl.

"No, just tired."

"All right." Fenton stood and shook my hand. "Hope everything goes good with that babe."

I smiled and nodded.

Fenton turned away. "Okay, Tyler, we'll talk to you tomorrow."

"See you guys tomorrow." I walked home, but not because I was tired. If I couldn't be with Ashton, I wanted to be alone.

Going into the dark, quiet house, everyone was asleep and I walked to my bedroom.

"Tyler?" Dad called from my parents' bedroom.

"Yeah?"

"Okay, just wanted to make sure it was you."

"Who else could it be?"

"Hey, your sister's coming in soon," Dad said, ignoring my question.

"Cool." I went to my room and wondered why my sister was coming home all of the sudden. But it would be nice to see her.

After changing into shorts and a t-shirt, I went downstairs to watch TV.

# 8.

I awoke on the couch the next morning exhilarated. The second night of the carnival weighed heavily on my mind and I was sure that if Ashton felt the same way about me as I did her, she'd be there.

Going into the kitchen, Mom was at the sink, drinking coffee. "Morning, Tyler. How was the carnival?"

"Okay, I guess."

She paused. "Everything good with Sander?"

Fixing my eyes on hers, I was dumbfounded by the question. "Yeah, Mom, everything's fine. Why wouldn't it be?"

She turned and put the empty cup in the sink. "Your sister's coming in tomorrow."

"Yeah, Dad said something to me about that. Why did I just hear about it last night?"

"We just found out ourselves yesterday."

"Oh," I said, suddenly curious. "Well, have a nice day at work."

———— ⌒ ————

After spending most of the day alone, I went to Sander's.

"Sup, Tyler," Sander said, answering the back door.

"Sup, Sander." I walked in. "Did you to talk to Tamara?"

"No man, haven't seen or talked to her since last night. Don't worry, though, she'll be there tonight."

I hoped that meant Ashton would be there too.

After watching TV a while, we went to Daryl's. Fenton quickly threw open the door after the first knock. "We don't want any!" he yelled, then abruptly slammed it. We laughed as Sander opened the door and we went inside. We talked for a few minutes then entered the car to head off. I thought one of the guys might bring up Ashton, but none did.

At the grounds, walking alongside Sander I tried not to make it look obvious that I was searching for anything. Daryl and Fenton once again went off with others.

As I walked with Sander, I heard my name. Turning, Clyde and Nate, two guys I'd known since I was in diapers, because our parents were long-time friends, appeared. Sander turned away.

Clyde and Nate were both skinny but Clyde wore glasses and was taller than Nate. "Hey, Tyler, what've you been up to?" asked Clyde.

"Um," I paused, glancing out the corner of my eye at Sander, who appeared anxious to keep walking. "You know, riding my bike. Sorry I haven't been around. Hey, do you guys know Sander?"

"Yeah, from school," said Nate, smiling.

"Tyler, I'm going to get going. Might get another 'Ride All Evening' stamp."

I knew that Sander was not up for associating with Clyde and Nate, and was sure they were not friends in school.

"Hey, I'll hook up with you guys a little later," I said, not wanting to seem rude or conceited.

Getting in line with Sander for the stamp, I expected him to say something denouncing my friends, but he didn't. Still, there was a perception that Sander didn't think highly of them.

Coming upon Tamara and Melissa, Ashton wasn't there. As Sander and Tamara chatted, I scanned the area, not finding Ashton.

"Hey, Tyler, what's up?" said Tamara.

"Hi, Tamara." I forced a smile.

Sander looked at me. "I think he's looking for Ashton."

"Oh, I haven't seen or heard from her since last night," Tamara said. "I don't know what she's doing."

"Yeah." I looked away.

"I don't know, she may show up," Tamara said, tenderheartedly.

I nodded. "It's cool."

She removed her cellular from her small blue purse. "I could try to get a hold of her. But, Tyler, didn't she tell you she has a boyfriend?"

My eyes widened. She didn't mention one and with the way she acted, I thought there might've been a future with her. After hearing this, I felt a little led on.

"No. I didn't know that." I disguised the hurt and letdown with a smile and a wave of the hand. "Don't worry about calling her."

"She's been saying how much she misses him."

"Come on, Tamara," Sander blurted. "Don't tell him that!"

"Sander, really, it's cool. Whatever."

Tamara then talked to Sander about the rides.

I turned away while they chatted, figuring Ashton probably wouldn't be here tonight. But I really wanted to see her, to find out the true story. Then I thought maybe she'd show up tomorrow, or the night after that.

Walking alone for a few minutes, I found Fenton and Daryl. "Sup Tyler? What happened to Sander?" asked Daryl.

"Oh, he's chilling with his girl."

"Where's your girl?" asked Fenton.

I thought about saying she wasn't my girl, but said, "I haven't seen her."

Fenton smiled, stood and removed the braid that was tying his hair behind his head. I followed the guys to the food stand. "We've been here almost an hour and Daryl is just now getting fries—got to be a record," Fenton joked.

"Hey, I can only get these fries one week a year, so I take advantage of it."

"Oh yeah, they're far superior to McDonald's fries," Fenton said.

"They are."

After ordering french-fries, we went to the pavilion where bingo was being played.

"We'll just sit at the edge here, not interrupting their bingo," Daryl said, sitting at the last picnic table on the pavement.

Three older ladies at the other end glanced at us.

"Just hanging out, eating fries with the senior citizens that play bingo all night," Fenton said.

Daryl and I laughed.

"Well, you know, that's what old people do," I said, expecting the guys to laugh again, but they didn't.

Daryl and Fenton talked and joked as we ate and I felt they were ignoring me and considered maybe they weren't really my friends. I wouldn't be with them if Sander hadn't come along. But Sander was not here now, he was with his girl, and I was just trying to not feel let down about Ashton not showing up.

Soon we got up and walked around. Nate and Clyde walked towards us. "Hey guys, what are you up to?" I asked.

"We just finished driving bumper cars and saw you," said Nate.

Daryl and Fenton laughed loudly.

I pretended not to sense their sarcasm. "Hey, this is Daryl and Fenton, neighbors of mine." I didn't call them friends. "This is Nate and Cly—"

"Yeah, what's up, guys?" Daryl interrupted, looking away nonchalantly.

"Okay," Nate said, bobbing his head, "I guess we'll see you later." He and Clyde walked away.

I walked with Daryl and Fenton, feeling as if I didn't belong with them.

Daryl turned back to me. "Why don't you go hang out with your friends?"

Sighing, I slowly turned away. "Fuck them guys, fuck them all," I muttered, thinking how arrogant and self-centered Daryl was. Then I searched for Clyde and Nate.

I found them in the Ferris wheel line. "Hey, dudes."

"Tyler," Clyde said, turning, "what happened to your friends?"

"They're not my friends," I answered, shaking my head. "They're my neighbors and they just gave me a ride here."

"You guys seemed like buddies."

There was a family of four behind Nate and Clyde, and I decided not to get in line. "I'll just hang out here while you guys go on this ride."

Nate nodded.

As they got on the Ferris wheel, I once again searched the surroundings hoping to find Ashton. But she was nowhere around. I saw Sander in the distance talking with two other guys, his buddies from school, I assumed.

When Nate and Clyde got off the ride, I wandered along with them. "So what have you guys been doing?"

"We've been here about two hours, just riding as many rides as we can," answered Clyde.

"The 'Ride All Evening' stamp is expensive enough," laughed Nate. "We have to get our money's worth."

"I hear you." Over the next half hour, I stayed with Nate and Clyde. Then they went to ride the bumper cars again and seemed interested in all the smaller rides, which I was not. I told them I was glad to see them and would call them. It got my mind off of Ashton for a little while. But now I was alone and didn't know what to do next. If I walked around and saw the neighborhood guys, they might've thought I was following them.

I was unaware of the exact time, but was certain it was after nine o'clock—maybe after nine-thirty—and twilight had turned to night. Believing it possible the guys left already, intentionally ditching me, I decided to just walk home. It was only a mile hike.

Crossing Quarles Road, I past a Circle K and a barber's shop and thought about how the night had not gone like I'd hoped. I was happy to find friends, but learned new things about Ashton and saw the true colors of Daryl and Fenton. Then I thought of how I used to get in trouble, hanging out with Jester and Rick, guys everybody told me to avoid, and how that made me an outcast. Even while not lying, stealing or smoking, I still felt in exile. Depressed, I continued walking home.

Not much later, headlights shined from behind me and a horn honked. Turning, I saw Daryl's car slowing down, then pulling over ahead of me.

I didn't know what to expect.

# 9.

Staring at the car, I trembled as Sander stepped out of the back. "Tyler, what are you doing, man?"

I just stared at him.

"Why the hell are you walking?"

"Uh, I was going home."

"We were looking all over for you! Shit man, why didn't you just find one of us?"

I didn't know what to say.

"Do you have a cell, man? I don't even have your number."

"No," I said. "I ain't got one."

"Come on. Get in the car," Sander sighed, climbing back in the car, leaving the door open.

I entered and closed the door.

"Tyler, why were you walking home in the dark?" Daryl asked with his unique snicker.

"You told me to go hang out with my friends. I figured you didn't want me around."

Daryl and Fenton both laughed. "Oh, man, we were just playing with you!" said Daryl. "Don't take everything so seriously."

I didn't believe that they had been joking.

Pulling into Daryl's driveway, Sander yawned.

"You tired?" asked Daryl.

"Yeah, yeah," Sander responded. "Think I'm just going to go to bed."

"No fire tonight?"

"No, Daryl, I ain't up for it." He exited the car.

I followed Sander to his backyard, hoping he would not bring up Ashton or my other friends.

"Tyler, think I'm going to hit the sack. I'm beat, man."

"Yeah."

"But hey," he paused, "we'll check out the carnival again tomorrow."

"Sounds good."

"All right, take it easy, buddy." We shook hands and I saw his weariness and wondered if the searching for me made Sander tired. But I laughed about it on the way home, thinking the guys were being good friends. It seemed like they were worried when they couldn't find me. I felt good about that and couldn't blame Sander for wanting to hang out with his girl over me. I would've done the same thing.

Entering the house, my parents were up watching television.

"How was the carnival?" Dad asked.

"Great!"

"Are you going again tomorrow?" Mom questioned.

"That's the plan." I sat with them to watch TV.

A little later my parents went to bed and I stayed up. Feeling better about the neighborhood guys gave me a hopeful perspective with Ashton. But then, I remembered being told she had a boyfriend.

# Part Two:
# A New Neighborhood

Justin Fleischman

# 10.

R iding across the street to the alley above Daryl and Sander's backyards, I glanced at the homes and thought about going to see Sander. After what happened last night, I hoped the guys weren't angry with me. Circling the bicycle at the dead-end, I again glanced at the houses then turned and rode up Gavy Lane and made a turn on my way to the playground, where Sander and I used to play basketball.

Passing the playground, a four-foot green chain-link fence surrounded the grounds. The basketball court was old and cracked. There were swing sets, a slide and a merry-go-round nearby, and a baseball field and a small green pavilion in the distance. I continued along the straightaway, thinking the place had shown its age and turned down a hill.

Coasting down Gavy Lane, I rode towards Sander's yard and dropped my bicycle at the yard's edge and went to the basement door. Sander answered after the first knock. "Tyler, hey."

"Sup, Sander?"

He looked back inside the house. His behavior seemed odd.

"Hey, I'm sorry I started walking home last night like an idiot." I flung my hand up. "I don't know what I was thinking."

Sander shook his head. "Don't worry about it. Hey, I'm kind of busy with something now. Can I talk to you later?"

"Yeah, that's cool. I was just riding my bike. Was up at the playground."

"You were up at the playground? Where we used to shoot hoops?"

"Yeah."

"Hey, go home. I'll be over in a few minutes. We'll play some b-ball."

"All right, sounds good."

"Okay, give me a minute and I'll be over."

He quickly closed the door and I still thought his demeanor was strange. I wondered why he told me he was busy then all of the sudden wanted to play basketball. Getting on my bicycle, I rode home.

Waiting outside the garage, Sander came dribbling a basketball. "All right, buddy, you ready to get beat?"

I bowed my head, laughing. "Yeah, we'll see." We headed up the road.

"It's been a while since we shot hoops together," Sander said, continuing to bounce the ball.

"That's true." I hoped Sander wouldn't bring up why we hadn't. It was something I wasn't ready to discuss with him "So what's going on tonight?"

"What do you mean?"

"We headed back to the carnival?" I swiped the ball from him.

"I don't know."

"I thought we were going to go every night. Have you talked to Daryl or Fenton?"

"Screw them guys!"

Taken aback, I wondered if his anger with Daryl and Fenton involved me in some way.

Bouncing the ball between his legs, Sander went to the free throw line and shot, making the basket. Grabbing the ball, he passed it to me. I rushed to the basket and missed a layup. Sander got the rebound and made a basket. Then we played one-on-one.

I guarded Sander as he drove to the basket. Turning to face me, he dribbled across his legs, went to the right and made a jump shot. Checking the ball to Sander, I faked a three-pointer and went to the basket. Sander guarded, pressing his forearm against my back, slightly pushing. I thought that a foul, but didn't call it. Trying to get around him, Sander's defense was too good. Eventually, I faded back, shot and missed.

Sander made the next basket. While I was on offense, Sander played intense, physical defense. Missing another shot, down 2-0, I decided to guard with the same aggressiveness throughout the game.

Sander won, 10-6, and I demanded a rematch. Sander accepted and we played very competitively with much pushing and shoving, but still had fun. It felt like it did when we were younger, and I forgot about the carnival, Ashton, Fenton and Daryl, and Sander's earlier oddness.

Sander again took the victory, 10–8, and we sat in the middle of the court, breathing hard. "Beautiful day," Sander panted, staring into the blue, cloudless sky.

"Sure is."

Sander rolled me the ball. "I'm not sure if I'm going to the carnival tonight."

"Not up for it?"

He paused. "I don't know. I might be there."

I smiled. "Well, let me know what you decide."

He nodded.

# II.

Upon returning home, my sister's car was in the driveway. Going inside, I saw her lying on the couch with her eyes closed. Her long, curly blond hair hung over the edge. "Hey Teresa, when did you get in?"

"I just got here, oh, about a half hour ago."

I again wondered what brought her to visit all of the sudden. Is she having trouble with her husband or job? Could she be pregnant?

"I'm tired," she said.

"Long drive?"

"That's it. Do you know when Mom and Dad will be home?"

"It'll be a few hours. They're at work."

"Right, it just seems later to me."

"So, what brings you to town?"

"I just had a few days off of work and I felt like coming home." She sat up on the couch. "Was feeling homesick."

I still wondered if she was having any problems.

"Here, come sit down, tell me what's been going on." She slapped the couch and I sat beside her.

"I was just playing basketball at the playground."

"Playing with anybody?"

"Yeah, Sander."

She smiled. "Mom told me you two have become friends again."

"Yeah." I looked away, not wanting to talk about our previous relationship.

"That's good. I'm glad you two have started talking again. Maybe he can be a good influence on you."

I almost laughed thinking with the people Sander's hanging around it might be the opposite. "You know the carnival's back in town."

"Yeah, that's right. That's why I planned my vacation this week. I thought I might bump into some friends there."

"We can check it out tonight, sis."

"Sounds good."

# 12.

I didn't hear from Sander and after eating dinner, went to the carnival with Teresa.

"Mom asked me the same thing you did." She started the car. "'What brings you in all the sudden?'"

I expected she'd tell our mother more than me.

"I told her I just wanted to come home for a few days."

I stared out the window, hoping she wouldn't park at the church, worried that, if we saw Daryl and Fenton, they could say something outlandish and crude, which was the same way I used to feel about her being around Jester and Rick.

She parked in the barbershop lot. We walked through the small, empty lot, across the main street and into the schoolyard. There was a new stand, "Dunk a Fireman," where you paid to pitch at a bull's eye to drop the fireman into water. A man's voice was loud in the half-filled pavilion, calling bingo numbers.

Teresa smiled, glancing at everything. "I used to have such good times here."

"What do you feel like doing?" I sensed the cheerfulness in her voice. "Want to ride the Ferris wheel?"

"Sure, in a little while. I just want to walk around first, see if I anybody I know is here."

"Sure," I said.

"Is Sander going to show up?"

"I don't know. He was being kind of weird earlier."

"Really? How so?"

"Well, first he wanted to be alone. Then, all of the sudden, he wanted to shoot hoops."

"Kevin!" Teresa yelled.

I turned and saw Teresa waving at someone smiling back at her.

"Excuse me, Tyler. I want to hear what you have to say. I just have to say 'hi' to someone."

Not offended, I followed her towards who I presumed was Kevin.

"Teresa Dyson, haven't seen you in a while," Kevin said with a grin.

"Well, I don't live around here anymore. And it's Williamson now."

"That's right. I'm sorry. I heard you got married. Any kids?"

"Not yet," she nodded. "Kevin, do you know my little brother, Tyler?"

He looked at me and I felt his with glance that he knew of my past problems. "Hey, Tyler." He extended his hand and I shook it.

Out of the corner of my eye, I saw Daryl and Fenton. They didn't notice me and I didn't bother gaining their attention.

Teresa hugged her friend goodbye and we walked along. She brought up how her and her friends used to stay out riding all of the rides until the place closed. I again saw Daryl and Fenton ahead, smoking, mingling with friends.

"Tyler! What's up?" Daryl called, motioning me to come over.

I peeked at my sister, then looked back at the guys, smiled, waved and kept walking.

"Come here, man!" Fenton yelled.

"Don't you want to talk those guys?" Teresa asked.

"I thought you wanted to ride something?"

"Well, we can stop and talk to our neighbors." She smiled, heading towards them.

On edge, I got ahead of her. "What's going on guys?"

"Just chillin'," Fenton said, blowing smoke from his cigarette.

"Hey, this is your sister, right?" asked Daryl.

"Yeah, Daryl. I remember you," She smiled.

I looked away, nervously, fearing the guys could behave crass.

"I ain't seen you in years, Teresa. Where've you been?"

"She lives with her husband, not around here," I quickly answered.

"Well, it's nice to see you again Teresa. Maybe you can stop over the Collinworths' for the bonfire while you're visiting. Oh, wait, I forgot, they're not having it anymore," Daryl said with false remorse.

"Yeah, that sucks," I quickly said. "I'll catch up with you guys in a little while." I turned and strolled away.

Teresa walked beside me. "Why's there not going to be a bonfire?"

"I don't know what he was talking about. Although, when Sander and I were shooting hoops, he seemed a little pissed at them guys."

After riding the Ferris wheel, we purchased drinks. Teresa asked questions about my homeschooling and what I had been doing with my time off. Then Sander walked past, alongside Tamara, with Melissa and Ashton trailing.

"Is that Sander?" Teresa asked.

"Yeah, that's him. Hey, Sander!" I waved him over, wondering why he didn't call me to say he was going to be here tonight.

Sander and Tamara came towards us but Ashton turned and spoke to Melissa.

"Hey, you remember my sister, Teresa?"

"Yeah, of course I remember Teresa. How've you been?"

They shook hands. "I've been good, Sander. It's nice to see you again."

"This is my girlfriend Tamara, and this is Ashton and Melissa."

"Hi!" Melissa smiled buoyantly.

I grinned and nodded towards Ashton. She smiled slightly then looked down.

Teresa continued talking with Sander and Tamara while Ashton and Melissa were whispering back and forth. Melissa then said something to Tamara and they walked away.

"Tamara, what did she say to you?" I asked.

"They just went to ride something."

"Hmm."

Sander looked over at the girls, walking away, then back at me. "Tyler, don't let her get away. Go talk to her."

Teresa laughed. "What? Does Tyler like one of those girls?"

"He likes 'em both," Sander joshed.

"I was hanging out with Ashton here the other night."

"Oh, yeah? Well, go talk to her then. I'll stay here and catch up with Sander. I haven't seen him in years."

Tamara was staring at me and I didn't want to appear eager to speak with Ashton. "I ain't going to chase her," I laughed. "But I don't feel like standing around. Think I'll just check out the carnival. Maybe dunk a fireman." Strolling away, I heard them laugh.

Passing where fries were being sold, Daryl called me and I noticed him and Fenton sitting on the bench. I walked towards them. "Sup?"

"Hey Tyler, when'd your sister get in town?" Daryl asked.

"How'd you know she doesn't live around here?"

"Because you just told me 'bout a half hour ago. Remember?"

"Yeah, that's right. Sorry."

Daryl and Fenton both laughed. "What's wrong, Tyler? Is Sander pissed at you?" asked Daryl.

My eyes locked on his. "What? No, I was just talking to him. Why would he be pissed at me?"

"He thought you were smoking and drinking in his backyard. Yeah, said you left empty beer cans and cigarette butts everywhere. He was pissed at you when I talked to him."

I stared at Daryl with narrowed eyes and clenched jaw. That explained why Sander was behaving awkwardly. I sighed in confusion over why Sander would've thought that and turned away.

Daryl and Fenton cackled again. Then Fenton said, "We're just playing with you!"

"Huh?"

"That was us, man!" Fenton laughed. "We were drinking back there. Now, Sander's pissed at us."

"Oh." I felt somewhat relieved.

"Yeah, he came over my place this morning asking me about it, saying his dad didn't want us having bonfires anymore. He knew it was us." Daryl laughed as annoyingly as ever then pointed his finger at me. "But his old man thinks it was you."

"Really?" I believed Daryl's comment could be true. "Well, that explains it. Thanks. I'll catch up with you later." I turned away.

"No, Tyler. Chill with us!" Daryl hollered. "Get some fries."

"Ain't hungry. I'll see you!" Continuing on, I heard them talking and laughing and didn't know, or care, if it was regarding me.

Walking around, I found Ashton and Melissa standing in line at a contest to win a goldfish and approached them. "Hey, what are you two up to?" I asked.

"I want to see if I can win a goldfish," Ashton smiled, not looking at me.

"Okay, good luck. Hopefully you'll do better than I did trying to win you a stuffed animal."

The stand with the round fish bowls was set up. Contestants stood eight feet away and had to throw ping-pong balls into one of the three small bowls to win a goldfish. Ashton handed the carnie a five. There was a small sign that read: One Dollar A Throw, Or Six Throws For Five.

She tossed underhanded and came up short on the first two, overshot the third, hit the glass on the fourth, made the fifth and under threw the last one. The man handed Ashton the clear bag of water with a goldfish and she smiled. I thought the cheap fish would be dead within a week but didn't say anything.

Turning, Ashton stared at the fish inside the bag. "Mom used to have a big fish tank with tons of different fish in it. She got rid of it after remarrying."

Walking along the crowded field, the rides were lit up and spinning. The girls chatted away and giggled, not acknowledging me. Realizing this night was not like the other one spent with Ashton, I just trotted away.

Feeling a little baffled and hurt, I found Sander talking with Daryl and Fenton, eating fries and laughing. I squinted, staring at them, wondering what was going on.

"Yo, Tyler!" Fenton called, seeing me walk up the knoll.

"Hey, sup guys?"

"You find your girl?" Daryl asked, tossing his empty fry container at a nearby trashcan.

I smirked. "Ain't my girl."

"Did you talk with Ashton?" Sander asked.

"Where's Tamara? Still hanging out with my sister?" I asked, ignoring Sander's question.

"I don't know where they're at. They're around somewhere. Were you talking to Ashton?" he repeated.

The question slightly annoyed me. "She's hanging out with that other girl." I shrugged my shoulders. "She ain't into me tonight."

"Bitches are like that sometimes," Daryl laughed. "You don't know what's in their heads."

I thought calling her a 'bitch' was harsh, but didn't comment. Then Sander and Fenton started busting on Daryl over all of the fries he'd been eating.

Daryl lit a cigarette and we started walking. The day's sunlight had faded and the carnival's attractions lit the night.

Weaving through the swarm of people, I saw another neighbor and nodded. Two young boys ran by carrying sparklers. We went to the hall where bingo had finished and sat on the rear bench. Daryl stretched with the cigarette in his mouth.

"So what happened to that girl you were with, Tyler?" asked Fenton.

"I don't know," I answered shortly, thinking how I just told them she wasn't interested in me.

Suddenly, Tamara, Ashton and a few other girls came by. "Excuse me." Sander stood and went towards the girls. I glanced at Ashton, who had her head down, like she didn't want to risk making eye contact with me.

As Sander stood talking with the girls, I hoped somebody would call me over. But Sander did not even glance at me. I looked around and saw my sister in the distance and got up and walked towards her without saying a word to Daryl or Fenton and only glanced at Ashton along the way.

"Hey, Teresa, you ready to go?" I somberly asked.

She turned to me. "Sure, whenever you're ready."

I just nodded, looking away.

"Something wrong, Tyler?"

"Nah, just getting bored."

"Where's Sander?"

"He's around."

Teresa tilted her head, looking at me, narrowing her eyes. I knew she was confused. "Whenever you want to leave, we'll get going."

"Okay, let's go." We walked through the lawn, saying nothing more.

# 13.

Just before brushing my teeth the next morning, I heard the doorbell and went downstairs.

Sander stood wearing a white, sleeveless shirt, holding a basketball. "Sup Tyler? You up for a little b-ball?"

"Yeah, I'll play. Just let me finish what I was doing."

"What're you doing? Something I shouldn't have interrupted?" He smiled.

I laughed. "No, I was just going to brush my teeth. Come on in."

Minutes later, we were on our way to the playground. Sander dribbled the ball then passed it to me. Bouncing the ball from one hand to the other, I wondered about Sander's good-friends-one-moment, angry-with-them-the-next relationship with Daryl and Fenton, and how to question him about it. Passing the ball back to Sander, we made a right on the narrow lane.

"Yeah, Tyler, sorry things ain't working out with Ashton," said Sander.

I wasn't expecting Sander to just randomly blurt that out. There seemed to be hesitation and remorse in his voice, like perhaps he shouldn't have said anything. She must've told him, or he overheard her say she wasn't interested in me. I couldn't be mad at Sander for that. If anything, Sander tried helping me with Ashton and I appreciated it. "It's all right, dude."

"Girls are screwed up."

I then thought maybe it was safe to ask about the guys. "So, what's going on with Daryl and Fenton?"

"What do you mean?"

"Well, it seemed like you were pissed at them. Then you're hanging out with them at the carnival."

Sander looked down, half-smiling. "Well, it's because of them that we can't have no more bonfires in the back. Those two dickheads left beer cans and cigarettes lying around."

"Yeah, I know. They told me about it."

"Oh, they did?" He paused. "My dad bitched a lot. But don't worry, dude. I know you had nothing to do with it. And if anybody blames you, I'll defend you."

Brining up my past angered me. I no longer had an interest in smoking or drinking anywhere, let alone in his backyard—and I believed he knew that. "Carnival again tonight?"

"Absolutely."

At the court, I checked the ball to Sander and we started playing. With the score tied at 2, I guarded tightly and Sander's elbow came up and caught me hard in the jaw. "Ouch, son of a bitch!" I pivoted away and held my chin.

"Oh, man, I'm sorry!" Sander yelled with a laugh.

I spat and quickly turned to him, cursing under my breath. I had the notion to tackle him to the ground and toss a fist.

"Are you all right? I didn't mean to hit you!"

I panted, but my anger diminished. Believing it was unintentional, I wasn't going to make a fuss over it. "Yeah, I'm fine. But that's a foul."

Sander chuckled.

My jaw was sore, but we continued to play. Part of me still wanted to knock Sander down and try to hurt him. But I reminded myself the jab was an accident.

Sander won 10-8 and we started another game. I was leading 3 - 1 when Daryl's car pulled up alongside the grounds. Daryl and Fenton came out and walked inside the fence.

"What brings you two out here?" asked Sander, bouncing the ball between his legs.

"We stopped over to see you, and your Pops said you was up here shooting hoops," answered Daryl.

I thought it quite brave of them to go over the Collinworths' after what they pulled.

"We're in the middle of a game. Do you guys want to join in?"

"What? Me and Fenton versus you two? We'd destroy you," Daryl said with his annoying laugh.

"Well," Sander smiled, "you can join in now. You guys pick who you want to team with."

Daryl shook his head. "How much longer are you going to be playing?"

"Want to just play to five?" Sander asked me.

"Sure," I nodded. "I'm all ready up 3 to 1."

"Okay, whatever," said Daryl turning away and following Fenton off the court.

Daryl and Fenton stood to the side, talking and laughing while we played and I wondered what they were speaking about and if we all would get along. It took my concentration off the game and Sander came back to win 5-4.

"Well, your undefeated streak against me stands. But we'll meet again!" I said high-fiving him.

"What, Tyler? You can't beat this scrub?" Fenton asked, as he and Daryl strolled onto the court.

I shrugged my shoulders.

"All right, time for two-on-two!" Sander dribbled the ball between his legs.

"Yeah, but first I want to run something by you, Sander," said Daryl.

Sander stared at him, wide-eyed.

"Since we can't chill in your backyard anymore—"

"Yeah, thanks to you two," Sander interrupted, bouncing the ball, looking away.

Daryl stood silent, staring at Sander, and I feared an unpleasant confrontation.

"Forget it." Daryl shook his head. "I can see you're still pissed about that. I'll talk to you about it later. Let's make teams."

"Well, if Tyler can't beat Sander, I don't want him teaming with me," Fenton said.

I stared at the ground.

Daryl nodded. "Then it's me and Tyler versus you and Sander."

"Sounds good to me," agreed Sander.

"Let's get it on, then." Daryl walked towards me and gave me a low five. "Okay, buddy, let's take these two to school!"

I smiled, feeling good about teaming with Daryl.

As we played, I was content with seeing everyone get along. We smiled and laughed, running hard and guarding close. But in the back of my mind I knew they hadn't made peace over the backyard incident and worried that if it was brought up again, there could be an argument.

Daryl and I won the game 10-9. "Yeah, Tyler! Told you we'd take 'em to school!" yelled Daryl.

"Okay, let's just see if you can do it again. Same teams," challenged Fenton, sweat dripping down his face.

"Sure, in a little bit," said Daryl, walking behind me and rubbing my shoulders.

As his fingers massaged my shoulders, I felt reassured that all of my old friends liked me again. "Yeah, I still haven't beat Sander one-on-one yet. But we'll meet again!"

Sander shot the basketball. "I'll wipe this court up with you anytime, Tyler. I bet I can beat everybody here."

"Don't talk what you can't back up, Sander," Daryl said. "Remember, you ain't never beat me."

"Anytime, Daryl. Anytime."

"Hey Daryl, what time did you want to head back to the carnival?" Fenton asked.

Sander bounced the ball to Daryl and he went in for a layup. "We'll head over about seven." He glanced at me and Sander. "That good for you two?"

We both nodded.

Daryl looked towards the road, then around the playground. "I used to have this friend, Bruce Morolski. We'd come here and smoke cigarettes, figuring we wouldn't get caught here." He paused "That was over five years ago."

"I remember Bruce," said Fenton. "Whatever happened to him?"

"He lived up near the old SuperSavings grocery store," Daryl continued, ignoring Fenton's question. "He'd get cigarettes from there."

"How'd he get smokes from there?" I asked.

"Bruce said he stole them, but I doubt it. Probably just had his older brother buy them."

We laughed.

"That's what I wanted to ask you guys about." Daryl paused. "Up the hill from Bruce's old crib, there's a clearing in the woods. We used to hide out up there. I don't think anybody knew we were up there chilling, smoking cigarettes. I was thinking we could go back up there and hang."

"Cool with me," Fenton said, shooting.

"But Bruce doesn't live there anymore?" asked Sander.

"Oh, hell no. He moved out years ago. I don't know where he's at now."

"Are you sure we can still go there?" Sander inquired. "It's not somebody's property, is it?"

"Sander, it's up the hill in the woods! Ain't in no yard."

"Okay, Daryl. I'll take your word for it." Sander stretched his arms behind his head.

"All right, same teams, let's play!" Daryl ordered.

Sander and Fenton won the game, 20-16. With perspiration flowing down our bodies, damping our shirts, we all got in Daryl's car and left the playground.

"Remember to be at Daryl's at seven, Sander," Fenton said.

I wondered why Fenton didn't include me, but didn't ask.

"Yeah, I'll be there," said Sander.

"Is your girl going to be there?" Daryl asked.

"I don't know. I left my cell at home and haven't heard from her."

Daryl looked in the rearview mirror at me. "What about your girl?"

I shook my head. "Ain't got one."

"Yeah you do!" Daryl bobbed his head, smiling. "What about that girl you were chilling with the other night? She seemed into you."

I shook my head and thought about Teresa. If she was going to go to the carnival, I probably should go with her, being that she was only in town visiting.

Instead of making a left down Gavy Lane to our homes, Daryl made a right.

"Where're we going?" I asked.

"There's been something I've been meaning to take care of for a while now," Daryl responded.

We drove to the very top of Gavy Lane and made a left on Thaxton St. This was a street I used to spend much time on. I closed my eyes and bowed my head as we past Jester's house and then Rick's house. I didn't even know if they still lived there, but I didn't want to take a chance on being seen by anyone on the street.

I lifted my head slightly and glanced out the windshield as Daryl pulled over. We were near the last house on the dead-end street. Trees went up a hill as the road ended.

"When I was younger, I used to hang out with Tyler's buddies Rick and Jester," laughed Daryl.

I grinded my teeth and my arms shook.

"The family that lived in this house had a Doberman pinscher that bit me about ten years ago. I had to go to the hospital."

"So what?" Sander asked. "The dog's not still alive, is it?"

"No. But they have another dog in the back."

"Okay," said Sander. "Another Doberman? You looking to get bit again?"

"It ain't a Doberman. It's a white and brown Coonhound." He laughed and his voice went to a softer tone. "I've been watching this house for a while now. And I'm coming back to see their other dog."

I glanced at Sander and then looked down. I knew that Daryl had thought up a twisted plan. Daryl reached into the glove-compartment. I again lowered my head, not wanting to see what he was removing.

"I'm coming back for revenge," Daryl said, opening the door.

As the three exited the car, I remained inside with my head bowed. After less than a minute, there was a light knock on the window.

I looked up and saw Sander. He opened the door and knelt down.

"You all right, buddy?" he asked.

"What the hell are they doing?"

He shook his head. "I don't know. I guess being their asshole selves."

As I opened my mouth to say something, we heard two light pops then a dog's howl. Sander ran around the car and I followed along the side of the small white house with blue siding to the back yard.

Daryl had a thick rope around the dog's neck. His face was red and he was biting his lower lip as he fought hard to crush the dog's trachea. The dog's head was shaking violently, trying to break free as Daryl continued to choke the life out of it. The dog's knees buckled and that's when I noticed two areas bleeding on its body and it collapsed. Daryl removed the rope and tied it around his forearm then picked up the pistol and placed it in his waistband.

I gasped as Fenton ran back towards us. "Hey, help us drag this dog into the woods."

I started shaking and looking to see if anyone else was around. "Why'd he do that? What's wrong with you guys?"

"Dog at this house bit Daryl, about ten years ago."

Sander and I were both silent.

Fenton's eyes widened and he flung his hand in the air. "One of you needs to help us drag the dog into the woods!"

"No!" I snapped. "I'm not helping you at all!"

Fenton looked at Sander.

"No way, man." He shook his head and took two steps back. "I had nothing to
do with this."

Fenton sighed and ran back to Daryl.

———————

Back at the car, I sat on the ground and leaned against the passenger's side back door and Sander stood near the trunk. I looked into the cluster of trees and overlapping hills in the distance. It was a nice view from up here, but all that this area seemed to bring for me was trouble. Then I glanced at the nearby houses, making sure that nobody was watching us.

After about ten minutes, Sander wanted to see what was taking the guys so long. I reluctantly followed him through the yard, because I didn't want to be alone.

Entering the woods, I followed Sander along a small patch surrounded by smaller, frail trees and bushes into the growth of larger trees.

Sander tilted his head to the left and gazed in that direction then walked up a hill. I assumed he heard something and followed. Then I heard Daryl's laugh.

Up on the hill we found the Coonhound hanging by a rope from a thick branch. Its tongue hung out and blood dripped from its mouth.

"You guys are sick!" Sander said.

"Me?" laughed Fenton. His plain white shirt was now filthy with splotches of blood. "I didn't shoot the dog with a BB gun and choke it out. I just helped Daryl hang the pooch."

Daryl spun the dog slowly and smiled, taking pride in what he had done. "This looks just like a deer after a hunter shot it, except it ain't gutted." He laughed. "Any of you want to help me gut it?"

I quickly turned and went down the hill.

Exiting the woods, Sander walked beside me. I expected him to say something, but he didn't.

"Think I'm going to just walk home," I said.

"Sure," he said. "I'll walk with you."

Daryl and Fenton ran to us. Daryl walked beside me, and Fenton was next to Sander. I pretended like I didn't know they were there.

"Sup guys?" Daryl laughed.

I didn't want to talk about what they had done and hoped they wouldn't bring it up.

Sander followed the guys to the car and so did I. As Sander got in the back I figured I might as well ride with them. It would be quicker and maybe safer than walking along Thaxton Street and possibly being seen by people that lived on this street.

Entering the car, I thought I should tell my parents what Daryl and Fenton had done or maybe just call the police myself. Because I was there and had been aware of the crime that they committed that automatically made me involved, and I certainly didn't need charges on my record.

"Yeah, those people are assholes anyway," Daryl said as he drove. "And there ain't a fucking dog I'm afraid of anymore. I weigh about 170lbs. No dogs, at least around here, outweigh me. I wish that dog would've bit me. I wouldn't lay there and cry, like a little bitch. I would've grabbed one of its legs and snapped it in half."

Not paying attention to Daryl, I thought how becoming friends with Sander again was something I was happy to have done. But Daryl and Fenton were out of control and terrified me. I didn't want anything more to do with them and I didn't want to think about what they might do next.

"Be at my place at seven," Daryl said, pulling into his driveway.

"Hey, if I'm not there, just go without me," I said, avoiding eye contact with them.

"What? You got something better to do?" asked Daryl.

I shook my head. "If my sister's going, I'll just head there with her."

"Oh," smiled Daryl. "I got a better idea. Why don't you go with Fenton and Sander and I'll go with your sister."

Fenton laughed and I sighed, thinking I didn't want Teresa anywhere near Daryl.

"I'm just playing with you, Tyler. See you guys later." He turned away.

As Sander and I walked through the yard, he said, "Yeah, Tyler those guys don't mean nothing by that--"

"Sander, it's cool. I know they're just fooling around." I didn't look at him and just wanted to get away.

"I just don't want you getting pissed."

"Don't worry about it." I wondered if Sander was as fearful of those guys as I was.

"All right, buddy." Sander stuck out his hand, smiling, and I slapped it. "If I don't see you at Daryl's, I'll see you at the carnival."

"Definitely."

I walked across the street quickly and went into the backyard. Shaking with fright, I didn't want to be at home or even in the neighborhood. I wondered if someone saw what Daryl did and called the police. I was scared a police officer could come to my home and question me about what had happened. And, because of my record, I might've have had a hard time convincing the police that I had nothing to do with it.

Then I imagined how the family might feel if they went into the woods searching for their dog and found it hanging. What if they had a child that was close to the dog? How would the child react seeing it hung from a tree? Still panting, I thought about how happy I had been a short time ago when we were playing basketball. It felt great teaming with Daryl, and we all got along. I thought my problems with those guys were in the past.

And then Daryl murdered a dog. He and Fenton thought it was a joke. And I was unsure how Sander felt about it. Maybe he was just as sick as those two.

About ten minutes later, I shook my head and thought I'd just try to forget about what Daryl had done

—maybe only because I had nothing to do with it. I just wished I would've stayed at the car and not followed Sander into the woods. Then I wouldn't have seen anything that had happened.

Coming into the house, Teresa was sitting at the kitchen table talking on her cell. "I just really wanted to come home for a few days. I miss my family."

Believing she was speaking with her husband, Robert, I didn't want to eavesdrop. I went into the living room, sat on the couch and turned on the television. After a few minutes, Teresa came in smiling. "Hey, Tyler, I didn't hear you come in." She plopped down beside me.

"I just got here. Was that Robert on the phone?"

"Yes," she nodded. "I thought I should give him a call."

I sensed tension. "Is. . .everything okay?"

Teresa pressed her lips together and her eyes widened. "Everybody asks that—him, Mom and Dad. I tell everyone the truth. I'm not having any troubles— it's just that I wanted to come home for a while. I wanted to see my family and friends."

"Oh." I felt a little baffled, believing she was hiding something.

"It's not really a problem with him," she firmly repeated. "I just feel lonely and bored, being miles away from home. I miss it here."

Placing my hand on her shoulder, I was unsure of what to say.

"I guess I'll just have to get used to it." She paused, looking away. "Things'll get better."

"If there's anything you need to talk about, I'm here."

"Thanks." She stared at me and I knew what she was thinking—how I'd matured and how far I'd come over the past year-and-a-half. I also believed my sister might've really needed me and it would be wrong to blow her off for guys I'd have probably been better off avoiding.

"Remember Rachel Conlon?" she asked. "I was talking to her yesterday and I was going to spend some time with her tonight."

"You're not going to the carnival?"

"Well, we may end up there. I don't know. Are you going tonight?"

I smiled and leaned back. "Yeah, I'll probably catch a ride with the guys."

"Is that girl going to be there?" She smiled, crossing her legs.

"I really don't care."

"Oh," she said. "Well, if there's anything you need to talk about, I'm here for you too." She slapped my knee, stood and walked into the kitchen.

# 14.

I went out into sprinkling rain, hoping it wouldn't shower harder, thinking that could damper the plans for the fourth night of the carnival. Adjusting my Steelers cap, I walked to Daryl's driveway. The guys were leaning against the car talking.

"Tyler, you made it!" Sander hollered.

"Yeah, I'm here."

"Ain't Teresa going tonight?" asked Daryl.

"She's hanging out with a friend of hers."

Daryl nodded and I was glad a crude remark didn't follow.

Sander turned to Daryl. "Well, we're all here. Do you want to take off?"

Daryl checked his watch then peered into the garage. "Yeah, let's to get going." He paused. "You know tomorrow they're going to have that stupid kids' parade before the carnival. I was thinking we could check out that place I was telling you guys about earlier."

We looked at each other, and Fenton said, "Sounds good."

"All right!" Daryl again glanced inside the garage. "Let's go."

The tires slowly moved along the gravel as we pulled into the church lot. Scattered raindrops fell and I heard rumbling in the distance. "Son of a bitch, sounds like a storm," Daryl said, shifting into park.

"Well," Sander sighed, "maybe it will pass us."

Daryl shook his head. "Don't count on it. It always rains at least a little during the carnival."

The sky was grayer and it began raining more. Still, we proceeded on our way and I wondered if showing up was even worth it tonight.

"Guys, with the rain and thunder, carnival's going to suck tonight. Nobody's going to be out," Sander stated.

I glanced at him in agreement.

Daryl smiled. "I got to get some fries."

Sander laughed. "Yeah, it'll suck and we'll get sick but at least you'll get french-fries, that'll probably get soaked because of the rain."

"He's probably right," laughed Fenton.

"You guys are the biggest pussies."

None of the rides were running in the schoolyard and we walked to the food area. Daryl bought a large fry and Sander, Fenton and I each purchased a small. They added vinegar and ketchup to theirs and I ate mine plain. Gazing at the surroundings, I noticed the area was bare compared to the first three evenings.

Sitting on a wet park bench, we heard another thundering boom. "Geffers told me he's going to have some tonight," Daryl said to Fenton, who smiled and nodded.

I believed they were talking about drugs and I turned to Sander. "Are we going to get another 'Ride-All-Evening' stamp?"

Sander put a fry in his mouth, chewed and shook his head. "Dude, I don't think it'll be worth it. All the rides are shut off and who knows if they're going to be turned on again."

With Daryl's comment, I forgot the rides weren't running and felt dumb for asking. Deep down, I just didn't want Sander going with Fenton and Daryl. "Yeah, I guess they won't be turning them back on. Carnival's a bust tonight."

Daryl stood, still eating. "So you guys want to just take off? Forget about it tonight?"

Sander turned to me.

"Fine with me. I'll just stay home," I answered instantly, not wanting to be involved in anything they might've had planned.

Daryl smiled. "Yeah, we'll just head home. Nothing else to do tonight."

I gawked in bewilderment, because that wasn't what I overheard him say he and Fenton were going to do.

The rain hadn't let up as we jogged to the car. Fenton and Daryl panted heavily along the way. Daryl unlocked the car doors and we got in. "Okay, me and Fenton are going to head to a friend's house."

"Yeah," went Fenton. "You guys want to come?"

Sander wiped his face then looked at me.

"Nah, just drop us off," I said.

"You sure?" Daryl asked, backing up.

"Yeah," I answered. "We'll just chill at home."

Fenton looked at Daryl. "Guess it's just you and me going to Geffers."

Seconds later, I heard Daryl on his cell. "Geffers, what are you up to?"

I looked out the window.

"Oh, you're downtown? Where?"

Daryl laughed as Geffers spoke. "Okay then, me and Fenton will be down in about five or ten minutes."

Nothing else was said on the way back and Daryl pulled into his own driveway. I thought, with the rain falling, he could've dropped us off at our houses. "Last chance to come with us," Daryl offered.

Sander opened the door. "That's okay. Thanks for the ride back though."

Fenton looked over his shoulder at me and smiled. "Carnival'll be better tomorrow night."

"Should be. Friday's always good."

As the car pulled out, we stood hunched in the rain. "Man, this rain's ruining our night." Sander flung his soaked, dripping hair back.

"Yeah, I'm going to get out of this. Want to come over?" I offered.

Sander didn't answer but followed me to my back porch. I smiled, as Sander and I stood under the porch roof.

"So, what's up now?" Sander asked.

"Guess we can just hang out here if you want. We can watch some TV or maybe play the Xbox"

Sander ran his hand through his wet hair. "Sure. If I go home, Tamara will probably call and want to talk all night. I'm not in the mood for that. If I'm hanging out with you, that'll give me a good excuse for not answering her calls or texts."

I chuckled.

We took our shoes off in the kitchen and Mom walked in. "Sander, is that you?"

Sander placed his shoes away from the door. "Yep! How are you, Mrs. Dyson?"

"Oh, I'm good. It's nice to see you again. You two are soaked! Let me get you some towels."

I thought it had been a while since Sander was inside the house and Mom probably remembered him how he used to look. "Yeah, Mom, the rain kind of ruined our plans. So we're just planning on hanging out here tonight."

Mom gave us towels. After drying off, Sander spent several minutes speaking with her. Then we played Call of Duty: Warfare 3 on the Xbox 360, talking and laughing loudly.

After playing the videogame, we watched television and reminisced about some of our adventures in the woods when we were younger.

"Remember the creek by the cemetery?" asked Sander.

"Well, the creek wasn't by the cemetery. There was a path near the cemetery that led down to the water."

"That's right."

"I haven't been there in years."

"Me neither. We should check it out. Maybe tomorrow?"

"Sure. We can finish the shed we started back in the day."

"I think we're a little old to be building a hut with sticks and mud."

"I was just kidding." I stared at him. "But I'm up for checking it out tomorrow."

Sander left around 10:30 and I was excited about our plans to go into the woods. It got my mind off Ashton and how she played me. Teresa came in soon afterwards and I went to greet her. "How's Rachel doing?"

"Good. We just talked at her house and had a few drinks. Did you go to the carnival?"

"Yeah, it sucked."

"Usually does with the rain. Hopefully it'll be better tomorrow."

We spoke for a few minutes then I went back into the living room, laid down and eventually fell asleep watching a Cheers rerun.

# 15.

The TV was still on when I awoke around 6:00. Shutting it off, I went upstairs to my bedroom, but couldn't fall back asleep. I was excited about going to the cemetery and creek, deciding if Sander wasn't interested in checking it out, I'd go by myself.

At 10:00, the sun was shining and I was sticking to my plans on going into the woods, with or without Sander. Dressed in an old pair of loose brown shorts and a worn-out white Pittsburgh Penguins t-shirt, I walked to Sander's.

Knocking on the basement door, Sander quickly answered. "My man, T-dog, what's up?"

"I was going to head to the cemetery and down to the creek. Want to come?"

"Hell, yeah! Come on in."

I went inside.

"Just let me get changed and we'll get going."

Minutes later, Sander trampled down the steps wearing a gray shirt and black sweatpants.

"It's a little warm out for long pants," I said.

"Yeah, I know. But if we're going to be going through thorns and weeds, I don't want to be in shorts."

"Yeah, right. I didn't think of that."

"If it doesn't rain again, the carnival should be better," Sander stated as we walked up Gavy Lane.

I was silent for several seconds before asking, "Tamara going tonight?"

"Don't know for sure. I haven't talked to her. But she'll probably be there."

I would've much rather just hung out with Sander tonight and avoid the females' drama as well as Daryl and Fenton.

We went beyond the road that led to the playground. Reaching the top of the hill, we past Thaxton Street and I looked away from it. The hill descended downward and we turned on a dead-end street that led into the woods where branches hung low. The walkway seemed narrower than it used to be. Going up a rocky uneven surface, we came to a large chain-link fence. The rear gate to the cemetery was locked, which it never was before. Panting slightly, we slipped our fingers through the holes in the fence and stared at the tombstones.

After several seconds, Sander turned away. "Not much changed here."

I glanced at him. "It's changed a little."

Sander shrugged his shoulders. "Maybe you're right. I don't remember."

Traveling alongside the wide gap between the fence and the forest, we headed deeper into the woods and followed a trail. The area was mostly dry, but there was a large pool of muddy water near the path's entrance. It zigzagged and a few more puddles were along the way. Other trails veered off into the timberland, but we remained on the one that led to the creek. The walkway got steeper as we approached the bottom where the shallow water flowed. Sander went to the brook's edge and smirked.

"What?" I asked.

"I don't know what we ever found so fascinating about this."

I stared at where rocks used to stick out and shade the base of the cliff. But boulders and dirt had caved the area in. "It's still kind of nice here."

Sander turned. "I guess. Maybe I just grew out of going into the woods." He laughed. "I mean, if I was alone with Tamara in the woods, that'd be different."

I didn't comment as we went back to the trail.

"Want to check out the witch's house?" Sander asked as we strolled out of the forest.

My eyes widened and I chuckled.

Sander smiled. "Bet you haven't thought of her in years."

The witch was a nickname for and elderly lady by the last name of McCough. Her house was small with chipped blue siding. Sander and I used to hide and throw rocks at the home and ring the doorbell and run away. The fad didn't last very long and we never got in trouble for it.

"I wonder if she's still alive," I said.

"Not sure," replied Sander. "But even if she is still living, I bet she ain't living there. She's probably in an old folk's home."

"Right."

We walked a little ways, making two rights on the back streets. When we got to the home, almost all of the blue paint had chipped away, a drain was hanging off of the place and the windows were cracked.

Sander shook his head. "Surprised this place hasn't been torn down."

"Right. It's beyond salvaging." I looked around, thinking the place appeared even worse than it looked when we used to come here and how rotten we were for playing tricks on the old lady.

"You ever been inside the place?" asked Sander.

"No." I looked down, shaking my head. "I've never been inside of there."

"I thought maybe old lady McCough might've let you in for milk and cookies and to see pictures of her grandchildren." He looked back at the house. "Hell, Tyler, let's look through the windows."

"What? There's nothing in there."

"Probably not. Probably just rats and opossums running around. But I'm curious."

Sander walked through the small yard and I followed.

The three steps leading to the porch creaked as we stepped on them and the boards that made the porch weren't any sturdier. Sander knelt down and looked inside the window.

"Anything interesting in there?" I asked.

"What do you think?"

I laughed.

"Hey, what are you doing over there!" someone yelled from across the street.

Turning to see who was hollering, my left food went completely through a board and I felt my leg being cut. "Shit!"

Sander bolted off of the rickety porch as I lifted my leg out of the hole and followed him.

After running around a corner and off of the street, Sander stopped, put his hands on his knees and laughed. "Are you okay?"

"Yeah, I'm fine." I stared at my leg and there was a thin cut about six inches below my knee and two other small cuts.

He continued to chuckle. "Guess somebody was pissed that we were over there."

"What's up with that? It's not like there was anything there we could've stolen."

"Right. How's your leg? You'd better check to make sure nothing crawled into your shorts and is moving around in there. You don't want it biting anything important."

I laughed and brushed dust off my shorts.

---

At 5:30, the sun shined and the weather appeared promising as I walked to Sander's backyard to find him sitting in a lawn chair before the flameless pit. "Sup, Tyler?"

"What's up?"

"I guess the plan's still on to check out that place Daryl was talking about."

I had forgotten about Daryl wanting to go somewhere before the carnival.

Sander stood. "Guess we can check it out." He proceeded to Daryl's and I followed, biting my lip and shaking.

Answering the door, Daryl glanced at his phone. "Right on time. Okay, we just got to pick Fenton up."

As Daryl drove up Gavy Lane, Sander rode shotgun.

Making a left on Orckon St., we pulled alongside the redwood fence at Fenton's house and Daryl honked the horn. Sander opened the car door. "I'll see if he's ready."

Fenton came out of the house and Sander turned back to the car and entered the back with me.

Fenton slammed the door. "I think I know where you're talking about."

Daryl glanced at him.

"I remember being there with you and Morolski back in the day."

Daryl started driving. "Yeah, you might've been there."

Going along the main street, Daryl made a left turn onto Sky Drive and followed it to the abandoned SuperSavings store and parked next to the building. It was white with green chipped siding and a flat roof. "Man, I used to have times here."

Sander opened the door. "Yeah, stealing cigarettes with Morolski."

"Nah." Daryl exited. "I never stole anything from here. That was all Morolski." Walking alongside the front of the building there were two large boards where the two glass doors used to be. "Me and Morolski used to look in at the cashier girls. We'd blow them kisses and stare at them, holding our crotches and licking our lips."

We laughed. "You never got in trouble for that?" asked Sander.

"Once, the manager came out and told us if we didn't leave he'd call the cops." He paused. "We left, but not before Morolski said: 'fine, call the cops. But I still owe that girl money from last night.'"

Moving away from the vacant building, we trotted down steep Fennor Street. Three houses lined the left and long grass grew near the woods.

"Morolski lived down here?" asked Sander.

"I'll show you. Let's cut through the woods." Daryl led us through shrubs. Large trees surrounded us along a narrow downward path. Turning, the trail got wider until it came out at a clearing. Daryl walked to its center where burnt debris lay. "This is where me and Morolski used to hang."

Fenton gazed at the surroundings. "Yeah, I've been here before."

I walked near where burnt wood lay in the center of the clearing. "Did you used to have a fire here?"

"Yep," Daryl smiled, "and it looks like it's still being used."

Fenton lit a cigarette.

"Come down here." We followed Daryl between a few trees, down a hill to a spot at the edge of the forest that overlooked a backyard and a small house with a wooden back porch and a picnic table. "That's the old Morolski house. Man, we had good times there. But after Morolski moved away I stopped coming up here."

I noticed Sander's smile and fed off it. Often, when he seemed overjoyed, I felt everything was okay.

Going back to the clearing, we sat around the burnt twigs. Fenton threw his cigarette butt away, put another in his mouth and handed Daryl and Sander one. I looked away, fighting the urge to smoke.

Daryl and Fenton spoke while I just gazed through the trees.

Sander lightly elbowed my arm. "Looks like the weather for the carnival'll be better tonight."

"Right." I stared at the cigarette pinched between Sander's fingers and decided to give in a little and kill my craving. "Sander let me have a hit of that."

Daryl and Fenton turned towards me. "You want a cigarette?" asked Fenton.

"No, not a whole one. I just want a hit of smoke."

"Okay." Sander passed me the cigarette.

I inhaled it and immediately started hacking.

Daryl and Fenton laughed as I handed it back to Sander.

"Guess you're not used to it," said Sander.

"No." I again coughed. "Not anymore."

"Hey, that's a good thing!" smiled Fenton, holding his cigarette aloft. "You don't need this crap."

Daryl continued telling stories about his times in the forest. After a bit, Sander asked, "You guys ready to go now?"

Daryl looked at his watch. "The parade is still going on. We'll get going soon though."

Daryl and Fenton talked about drinking and I just smiled. As they smoked cigarettes, I felt tempted to ask for one again, but didn't.

Not much later, we proceeded up the path. Exiting the woods, Daryl and Fenton continued speaking amongst themselves.

I saw a man step out from the second house after the woods. He watched us as we ambled up the road.

"Nice place. Seems to have some sentimental value for Daryl," I said to Sander.

"Yeah, he likes it."

Driving to the carnival, we were stuck behind a Chevy Avalanche. Daryl grouched and I assumed the traffic was due to the winding down of the parade.

Turning into the church lot, Fenton put another cigarette in his mouth. Exiting the car, he offered one to Daryl.

"Not yet. I need fries first."

Fenton put the cigarette back in the box.

At the grounds, the rides were lit up and children and adults were sparse. We purchased fries and sat on a park bench. I looked at Daryl. "Why didn't you want to see the parade?"

Daryl shrugged, chewing on a fry. "I liked it when I was a kid. Now it's kind of boring. I just grew out of it."

As dusk settled, more people arrived and we weaved in and out of crowds. I thought Daryl and Fenton might go off by themselves, but we all stayed together.

Going alongside a noisy booth, where kids shot at bottles and bells rang, Ashton, Tamara, Melissa and three other girls stood. Tamara walked out and hugged Sander, then locked lips with him for a long, passionate kiss.

Daryl smiled and nodded. "Whoa, I don't think Sander's going to want to chill with us tonight."

"Yeah," agreed Fenton. "I don't think those two will even want to stay at the carnival tonight."

Sander looked at them grinning, then smacked Tamara's rear and rubbed it.

I saw Ashton in the bunch and turned away.

"Hey!" Ashton yelled, walking out from the girls.

I turned towards her as she came closer and got inches from my face.

"This is my man, right here."

I stiffened as she stared into my eyes.

"How've you been, Tyler? I haven't talked to you in a while."

I smiled as her midsection came closer to mine.

I leaned forward to kiss her and she slowly twirled around, leaned into me and shook her hips. I placed my hands around her smooth stomach and down to her hips, and she turned away again.

"Down boy," she slowly mouthed. Stepping back, she puckered her lips and blew me a kiss.

I stared into her eyes as she slowly backed towards her friends with her mouth slightly open. Confused by her behavior, which was completely different from a few nights ago, I continued watching her.

"Go get her!" shouted Fenton. "Don't let her get away. She wants it!"

Daryl and Sander laughed.

Sander and Tamara held hands. I repeatedly glanced at Ashton, who talked and laughed with her girlfriends near the food stand, not acknowledging me, while Daryl and Fenton ate fries. Everyone was smiling and chattering, except me and I felt left out. Taking another peek at Ashton, I could barely contain my desire to speak to her. But I knew her actions earlier where just a show for her friends and I believed if I spoke to her, she'd blow me off.

Suddenly, Daryl approached her, smiling, then whispered into her ear. She laughed and my eyes narrowed. Not wanting my emotions to show, I turned away.

Daryl was still speaking with Ashton, who was smiling and laughing. I edged towards them, trying to hear their conversation. Then, the two trotted away, laughing. My hands clenched and I bit my lower lip, thinking how Ashton teased me earlier. Daryl's walking away with her felt like a betrayal of our friendship, if we were even friends. Filled with resentment and anger, I wanted to do something out of the ordinary.

"Hey Fenton, let me bum a smoke," I said.

"What?" Fenton turned towards me. "You want a cigarette? Man, you guys are always bumming off of me."

"I never asked you before."

Sander turned to me. "Tyler, you were hacking a lung out before. You sure you want a cigarette?"

Fenton handed me one and lit it. Inhaling, I coughed.

"Tyler. . ." Sander's arms waved in confusion.

I turned to him and his eyes were wide open and his mouth slightly open. "I'll catch up with you later." I walked away, knowing my hurt showed.

Continuing on, taking puffs off the cigarette, I saw Nate and Clyde, but turned away from them. I considered my relationship with those two guys and how they behaved unlike the kids in my own neighborhood. I thought I didn't fit in with any of them. Sitting on the curb, I continued to smoke, coughing after almost every inhalation.

Teresa suddenly walked towards me with Rachel Conlon. I didn't want her seeing me smoking—she might tell our parents—so I swiftly flicked the cigarette away.

"Tyler, what're you doing?"

I smiled. "Nothing much."

She stared at me. "Something wrong?"

"No, I'm just waiting for Sander and his girl to get off the rollercoaster," I lied then looked at Rachel. "Hey, Rachel, how are you?"

"Good," she smiled. "How are you?"

I nodded. "Getting by."

"Tyler!" Sander yelled.

I stood and turned to find Sander coming over. "Hey."

"Why'd you disappear like that?"

I looked down, avoiding eye contact with both Sander and Teresa. If Teresa didn't know I was fibbing before, she surely knew now. I shrugged and coughed again. "I just felt like walking."

"Hey, Sander," Teresa nodded. "Having fun tonight?"

"Yeah, it's all right."

Teresa stared at me. I just turned away, knowing she knew something was bothering me. "Okay, we'll see you boys later." Teresa and Rachel walked away.

"Why'd you leave?" Sander asked. "It seemed like you were pissed."

I wondered if Sander already knew the answer. Then again, maybe he hadn't seen Ashton walk off with Daryl.

"Was it Ashton?"

I looked at him, but played down my feelings. "No, I don't care," I murmured.

"What'd you say?"

"No, nothing's bothering me."

"I can't understand your mumbles. Speak up. If you have something to say, say it loud and proud!" Sander laughed, smacking my shoulder.

I grinned back at him. "I'm fine. Let's walk around."

Sunlight diminished as we moved through the crowds. "Tyler, you shouldn't start smoking again," Sander said.

My head turned slightly. "What?"

"That smoking crap's no good. I only do it when those idiots Daryl and Fenton light up. But I'm going to quit. Tamara don't like it."

"That's good." I felt close with Sander, and could talk to him in ways I knew I could not with Daryl and Fenton. "Where's Tamara?"

"Chilling with her friends."

I wanted to ask Sander if he knew where Ashton and Daryl disappeared to, but didn't. "Want to ride the Super-Spinner again? It's the best ride here."

Sander turned to me. "Sure, let's get in line."

"So how do you like being homeschooled?" Sander asked as we entered the chambers.

My head turned rapidly, not expecting that question.

Sander grinned. "I mean, you've been homeschooled for a while now. Nothing wrong with that, but if you want to come back to school with us, that'd be cool."

I bowed my head, mystified over Sander's demeanor, then wondered if anybody in the public school would've forgotten my reputation. "Maybe someday I will."

"Yeah, Tyler, if you come back to school with us, maybe we could get practiced up with basketball at the playground and try out for the team this year."

"That'd be cool." I meant that, but doubted I'd ever be good enough to be on the school's basketball team.

"Or, I don't know, there're other sports we could play. I'll knock the smoking off and maybe we could go out for the swim team or run track. There's tons of shit we could do."

I smiled and we plopped into the warm plastic seats and the ride started.

As the cars slowed to a stop, the doors released and we exited onto the walkway. Coming down the steps, I saw Ashton wandering alone. "Hey, Ashton!"

She turned, smiled and kept walking.

"Want to ride something else, maybe the Ferris wheel?" Sander asked, surely trying to cover the slight.

I shook my head.

"Forget about her, dude—she's nuts."

I took a deep breath. "Nuts enough to run off with Daryl."

Sander sighed. "Yeah, I didn't notice they left together until after you took off."

"Where'd they go?"

"They just walked around together." Sander paused. "Listen dude, she's crazy. You'd have to be to spend so much time in one area, then go to a completely different place with another family and different friends."

"What the hell are you talking about?"

"You know, her parents are divorced. She spends most of the year with her mother then gets shipped off miles away to her old man for the summer. That'd be rough."

"Yeah." I winced and sighed in sympathy. "I forgot about her just being here for the summer. Sounds like you know about these things."

"Well, I have cousins and friends with divorced parents and I hear stories."

Sander led the way to the Ferris wheel and my thoughts drifted away from Ashton and to Teresa, knowing she would question my lie.

"This ride's the second best here. I like the Super-Spinner best," Sander commented as we approached the Ferris wheel. "The rest are sucky kiddie rides."

"Right."

The Ferris wheel started and the carts went up. Reaching the top, we stared at all the stars overhead, the car headlights coming and going and the colorfully lit carnival attractions. I smiled, thinking everything looked appealing from this height.

When the ride finished, we bounced down the midway to the grass. Searching the grounds, we soon found Daryl and Fenton.

"Sup Sander? Sup Ty?" Fenton said.

I was seldom called "Ty."

"What've you two been doing?" asked Sander.

"Me!" Fenton raised his palms. "I'm just chilling. I bumped into Daryl a minute ago. Yeah, him and Tyler's girl were off in the bushes."

I looked down.

"Yeah, and Fenton tried to get involved. But she didn't want anything to do with eggroll dick!"

Fenton faked a laugh and I continued to gaze at the dead grass, pretending I didn't hear them.

"Nah, we was just talking," said Daryl. "I ain't moving in on Tyler's lady."

That didn't ease my mood.

"You can quit being assholes. Just shut up about it," Sander interjected.

Daryl laughed. "Watch who you call an asshole. I could kick your ass for that!"

I knew that their hazing one another was done in humor and friendship. But I wondered how Sander could even stomach these two.

Ambling through the back road lit by the street lights, we went to the church parking lot. "Well, there's nothing to do now," commented Daryl.

"We got things to do, Daryl," blurted Fenton.

I figured they were talking about alcohol and drugs and didn't comment.

Ten minutes later, Daryl pulled the car into his driveway. We were all silent and Daryl looked bug-eyed in his rearview mirror at Sander and me. "What? You guys coming?"

"No." Sander shook his head. "We'll see you tomorrow."

We exited the car and I watched Daryl back up and drive down the street. I'd hoped Daryl would've told me more about the walk with Ashton. But if he said anything, whether it would've be something I'd like to hear or if it was discouraging, I wouldn't know if it was true.

"Tyler, what are you doing?" Sander asked, watching me stand still in the driveway.

"Nothing." I turned to Sander. "Just wondering where they're headed."

Sander said nothing.

"What are you up to now?"

"Listen, Tyler, Daryl ain't moving in on Ashton. He might want to, but trust me she won't have anything to do with him."

"Whatever, dude. I don't care."

"Daryl's an asshole. I know Ashton doesn't want anything to do with him."

I stared at him, curious as to how he knew that.

"I've told Tamara too many stories about the crazy shit that Daryl's done and she ain't going to let one of her friend's get mixed up with that freaking nut."

I wondered if Sander mentioned to Tamara about the time he kidnapped a baby and placed it inside a random car or more recently when he killed a dog. I was sure that would've shocked her.

"I'm just going into watch some TV now, I guess. What about you?"

I thought about my sister. She probably saw me with the cigarette and I wondered if she'd say anything to our parents. I deemed it a good idea to get to her before she talked to them. "Okay, dude. I'm going to see my sister. I don't know when she'll be leaving."

Teresa was watching television when I entered the house. "Hey, Teresa! When did you get in?"

"'Bout five minutes ago." She stared at me. "Everything okay?"

I bit my lower lip, nodding. "Sure. Why wouldn't it be?"

"Seemed to be a little friction between you and Sander."

"No, not really." I avoided eye contact with her, pondering what to say next.

"Well, I hope you're not doing anything that could get you into trouble."

"No." I looked into her eyes. "Sander's been a good friend to me."

"Okay," she nodded. "Well, I'm heading back tomorrow."

"You are? You're not staying for the last two nights of the carnival?"

"I want to have a day to recuperate before going back to work." She paused. "Try to make the best of my new surroundings. But I wish I could stay a little longer."

I nodded, unsure of what to say. "Well, I'm going to get a shower. Then I'll be back down to join you."

She smiled. "Thanks, but I think I'm going to turn in soon. Got a long drive tomorrow."

"I'm happy you used your vacation time to come and visit. Thanks for stopping." Going upstairs, I believed Teresa did see me smoking, but doubted she'd tell our parents.

Exiting the bathroom after showering, I heard Teresa talking in her bedroom.

"Rachel, I think that's bullshit."

I couldn't help but listen.

"Just leave. You don't need to be dealing with that!"

Silence.

"I'm not judging you. I'm here to here to help--"

Silence.

"Well I'm leaving in the morning. So I need you to promise me that if he ever pulls that shit on you again, you'll get out. Don't let—"

Silence.

"Well, just call if you need anything. Goodbye." She sighed after hanging up.

I crept towards the steps.

"Tyler, is that you?"

I turned back and went inside her room. She was sitting on her bed holding her cell.

"Tyler, were you eavesdropping?" she asked sitting on her bed.

"No. I just came out of the bathroom and heard you on the phone."

"And that's when you started eavesdropping?"

I bit my lip. "I just got out of the shower. I wasn't listening to--"

"Tyler, come here." She moved over on the bed and hit the mattress.

I just stood at the bed's edge and stared into her eyes.

"I was telling you the truth. I was feeling homesick and wanted to come home. But I also came back for Rachel. Her husband, Todd, well, he's been having mood swings. Sometimes she could tell when something was bothering him and he wouldn't tell her. And now it's gotten a lot worse. He's starting to hit her."

My jaw dropped and I gasped.

"She said, 'He always apologizes afterwards and she says everything's okay for a while. Then all of the sudden, he starts back up.'"

I turned away shaking my head, wondering why she was telling me this, especially after just treating me as if I was invading her privacy. I thought maybe she couldn't keep it in any longer and needed to say something to someone. It also made me think of the time I almost punched her and the guilt set in.

"Don't tell Mom and Dad I told you about this."

I nodded and exited her room. I'd never met Rachel's husband and knew nothing else about him. But I was sure I didn't like the guy.

# 16.

Around 11:00 am, Teresa placed her suitcase in the backseat of the car. She turned to Mom, gave her a hug then embraced Dad.

"You can always call if you need to talk to us," Mom said.

"Yes, I know." She released Dad and moved to me. "I love you all." She got inside her car.

"Love you, too," Dad said. "Call us when you get there."

When she pulled out of the driveway, I again thought of the cigarette incident and felt rotten. Teresa had seen me strive so far, and that surely appeared like regression. But I thought mostly she was concerned with Rachel and her wellbeing.

A little later, I dressed in shorts and a t-shirt, grabbed my basketball and proceeded up Gavy Lane, thinking about everything that happened over the past several days: Becoming friends with Sander again; Teresa's mysterious return home; The fear I had felt over witnessing what Daryl and Fenton had done and the path they might be leading me down; and meeting Ashton, a girl I really liked. She seemed into me sometimes and other times not so much. Maybe it was because she understood what I couldn't, that there was no future together. Through it all, I'd drifted apart from my long-time friends, the guys who'd been with me through thick and thin, Nate and Clyde.

Walking up the grassy slope and around the fence to the court, I dribbled the ball between my legs, shot a three-pointer and missed. Recovering the ball, I made a layup.

After shooting around for close to an hour, I came back down Gavy Lane, still thinking about my friends and family. Going through the garage, Mom was in the kitchen.

"Tyler, did Sander find you?"

"Sander? No. Why? Did he stop over?" I thought by her demeanor that something was wrong.

"Yes, he said he needed to talk to you. I told him you were up at the playground."

"Is there a problem?" I didn't mean to ask that aloud.

"That's what I asked. But he didn't answer." She paused "He sounded nervous."

"Okay." Turning away, I stomped back downstairs to the garage and outside.

Jogging through Sander's backyard, I pondered why Sander hadn't come to the playground and if the trouble had anything to do with Daryl and Fenton.

I knocked harder than intended on the backdoor.

Sander threw it open. "What are you banging so hard for?"

"Ahh," I paused, staring at Sander. The television was on and Daryl and Fenton were sitting on the couch, smiling at me, and it didn't seem like there was a problem. "I heard you stopped over," I gasped. "I was just shooting hoops. You could've—"

"Are you hyperventilating?" asked Daryl, still smiling. "Chill out. Everything's cool."

I came inside, not knowing if I should've been angry with Mom or Sander.

"I was just going to let you know, Daryl wanted to go back up in the woods before the carnival."

"Yeah, and we've been waiting for you," said Fenton.

"You guys want to leave now?"

"No," laughed Daryl. "Fenton's just messing with you. We'll get going around five."

"Come in, Tyler. We're just chilling." Sander walked forward and flopped in the brown recliner.

I wondered if Sander was purposively making it seem like there was trouble. Or perhaps it was regarding something he didn't want to discuss around Fenton and Daryl.

---

At 4:45, nobody answered after three knocks at Sander's backdoor so I circled the house towards the front.

"Tyler!"

I turned and saw Fenton motioning me to come to Daryl's and I briskly jogged over.

Getting to the front of the house, Sander was leaning against Daryl's car.

"Where'd Daryl go?"

"He's in the house," answered Sander.

Daryl strolled out of the garage with a six-pack of beer.

"Okay, Tyler's here. Let's get going." Daryl entered the car and placed the cans on the passenger side floor as Fenton got in. "I got to pick up more beer before we go into the woods."

I wondered where he was going to get beer and thought how nonchalant they were with their drinking while I was fighting a hankering for it.

"I swiped two twenties from my mom's purse," said Daryl. "She'll think she spent it on her own weed. You know what we got to do, Fenton."

"Yeah, I do."

I didn't know what they had planned. Looking at Sander, I didn't think he knew either.

———— ⚬ ————

We drove a few miles on Quarles Road and came upon Antonie's Italian Dining. Daryl pulled up a slope into the large square-shaped lot across from the restaurant that held several parking spaces and only two cars were there.

Daryl pulled into the far corner space and looked back at us. "You guys want to chip in?"

I wasn't going to give Daryl any money.

"No," said Sander.

He turned to Fenton. "What about you?"

"Daryl, you have forty bucks. That's plenty."

"I hope so." He stepped out of the car, walked through the lot and crossed the street.

"What's he doing?" I asked.

Nobody answered and I saw Daryl standing about ten feet away from the restaurant's door. After a few minutes, somebody walked out and Daryl talked with him, showing the money. The man shook his head and walked away.

A little later, two ladies walked to the entrance. Daryl spoke to them and they just walked inside the restaurant.

"Shit," said Fenton. "We did this before with no problem. First person we asked got us beer. People usually don't mind because we tell them they can keep the change."

A blue Ford car pulled into the parking lot and parked a few spaces down from us. Daryl raced across the road. "Excuse me!"

A skinny guy with a big nose and flattop stepped out.

As Daryl talked to him and showed him the money he just laughed then walked towards the restaurant. Daryl came back to us.

"These people are all fucking assholes." He sat and turned on the ignition. "We ain't getting no beer at this freaking yuppie bar." He opened the glove compartment and removed a knife with a sharp blade and long black handle. "But that dude's going to wish he bought us some."

"What're you going to do?" I asked.

He got out without answering and Sander and I looked out the back window, watching him walk to the car. He quickly shoved the blade into the two rear tires. I looked at Sander. His mouth was wide open and I knew he was as shocked as me.

Daryl then jogged out of the parking lot, grabbed a rock, came to the back of the car and threw it at the rear window, cracking it.

"What the fuck!" I said.

Fenton laughed.

Daryl ran back to the car, got in and backed up then quickly pulled out of the parking lot, tires screeching.

"I told you that asshole's going to wish he bought us beer," Daryl said.

I looked at Sander. His head was bowed and cocked to the side. Even when spending time with Rick and Jester, I had never witnessed such crimes as Daryl committed.

---

Making a left off the main drag, we drove to the abandoned grocery store. After pulling to a stop, Fenton stuck a cigarette in his mouth and stepped out. Daryl grabbed the beer and followed.

I noticed the several homes in the nearby area. With my heightened paranoia, I wondered if anybody would question why a car's parked here. Reaching the dead-end, we circled a bush and two large oaks entering the path that led to the clearing.

Daryl set the six-pack down and snatched a can along with Fenton. "You guys want one?" he asked.

Sander shook his head. "Nah."

"Good! There ain't enough for you two."

Fenton smiled while taking a sip.

Sander was silent. I thought he might've been as nervous and scared as I was.

Fenton tossed out his cigarette, took two out of the box and handed one to Daryl.

"You could let me bum one of those," said Sander.

Fenton sighed and handed one over.

I looked down, fighting the craving to smoke. I thought of my sister, and how disappointed she appeared when she might have discovered me smoking.

Daryl sipped his beer. "Ain't done this up here in a while."

Looking at Daryl, I hoped for his sake, the owner of the car he had vandalized wouldn't give an accurate description of him to the police. I thought he'd surely know that Daryl did it.

"You guys interested in the dance tomorrow night?" asked Sander.

"Oh, that lame dance. Are you kidding me?" Fenton slowly stood and walked to the surrounding trees and tore down thin branches.

"Dance?" I questioned. "Where's there a dance?"

Sander removed his cigarette. "There's a dance on the last night of the carnival. It's thrown by the fire department."

"What the hell are you doing?" Daryl asked Fenton.

"Getting twigs together to start a little fire."

I could not remember anything formal at the carnival before but realized if Ashton was present, it would most likely be my last chance with her.

Fenton carted over an armful of sticks and leaves and dropped them on the scantly grass-covered area.

"Why do you want to start a fire?" asked Daryl.

"I don't know." He shrugged. "To make us feel like we're in Sander's backyard." He removed a bottle of lighter fluid from the pocket of his baggy shorts. "That's why I brought this shit."

I bit my lower lip and looked down, hearing Daryl's squeaking laugh. I thought the place wasn't secluded enough for a fire.

"Tyler, I bet you want to dance with that honey tomorrow night," said Fenton, stacking leaves over the sticks, then squirting the fluid and attempting to light it all with his cigarette lighter.

"No, I think Daryl wants to dance with her," I responded, playing down my feelings and hopes.

"It's all right, dude," said Daryl. "I got all I need from her. You can have her now."

Sander turned to me and slightly shook his head and I said nothing.

Flames burned the debris, sending up a little smoke. Fenton turned to us. "Need more twigs to keep this going."

Daryl removed his cigarette. "Geez, Fenton, let me give you a hand." Standing up, he strolled downward towards the trees.

"I don't think this is such a good idea," I said to Sander.

Sander hunched over and tossed his cigarette into the fire.

Daryl shook the frail trees from below us near the forest's edge.

"Why are they doing this?" I asked.

"I guess because they want to."

When Fenton returned with twigs, the fire had begun dying down and he added the leaves and sticks. Daryl returned with more branches and larger pieces of wood.

Moments later, the small fire burned and Daryl and Fenton drank their second beer. Fenton removed another cigarette. "Before any of you ask—no!"

I heard an engine and the noise was growing louder.

Daryl's eyes bulged. He stood, dropped his beer then kicked and trampled on the meager fire.

Fenton and Sander dashed up the path and I followed, soon overtaking Sander.

Rushing out of the woods, I still heard the rev of the engine. Going up the street, I turned and found Sander jogging a good distance behind. Sander stopped when he reached me and rested his hands on his knees, breathing heavily. Daryl came running past us. Then I noticed the man I saw before, walking through the yard towards us. "Shit!" I yelled, fleeing.

"Damn, we left the beer," Fenton complained as we all got up the hill and leaned against the building, panting.

"What happened? You were right beside me. How did I get out of the woods before you?" I asked Sander.

Sander took a deep breath. "I went back—to find Daryl—make sure he was all right. He was hiding behind some bushes up the hill, staring at the guy that came up on a quad. The guy put out the rest of the fire, grabbed the beer then looked up and saw me and I just bolted."

"He saw you and Daryl?"

"Guy yelled, 'If this happens again, I'm calling the cops.'"

I trembled, heaving a sigh. "Let's just get out of here."

"We're all right now, dude. He didn't say he was calling the cops now." Sander went over and lightly punched Daryl on the shoulder.

# Part Three:
# New Neighborhood
# Trouble

# 17.

What the hell are these guys dragging me into? I thought trembling slightly as Daryl drove. Music blared loudly as we went along the main street with little traffic then pulled into the church lot. Exiting the car, I stayed behind as they meandered along and thought about the consequences had we been caught. These guys had never been punished—at least not like I had been.

Fenton turned. "Hey, Tyler, come here."

I slowly walked towards him. "What?"

"I'm going to help you with that babe tonight."

Biting my lip, I looked down.

Treading off the sidewalk, uphill on a back road passing the municipal building and houses, we entered the carnival. Fried food smells permeated the dry air as we past a game to win stuffed animals to the concession stand. I just stared at the rides while the other three each purchased fries. I was hoping to see Nate and Clyde, so I could just disappear with them. But I continued on with the guys after they bought their food until we came upon a gathering of girls, appearing to be in their late teens or twenties. Daryl and Fenton spoke with them. Sander stood away and I was even further back. Sander turned, shaking his head and rolling his eyes.

"What's up?" I asked, following.

"Let's get out of here." Sander moved along.

"What's going on?"

Sander continued shaking his head. "I'm not going to be around those idiots while they try to talk to girls."

"What'd they say?" I asked, imagining they were speaking inappropriately to the girls.

Sander didn't answer.

"Does it bother you when they act that way?"

Sander sighed. "Hey, that's them. As long as it doesn't reflect on me, it's no skin off my cock."

I laughed so hard I choked.

Sander smiled. "You okay?"

"Yeah. I just never heard that before."

Sander held out his almost empty fry container. "Want a fry?"

"Thanks." I took one and we strolled along.

Minutes later, we sat on a park bench and Sander looked around. "I really love summer."

I nodded and smiled.

"I like coming to the carnival, too. It's not as fascinating as it was when we were younger. The rides seem a lot smaller. I guess I just like the atmosphere and it staying light out until 9:30."

"Beats the winter when it's cold and dark at 5:30."

We recalled some rides the carnival used to have, and after a couple minutes, Tamara and Ashton approached us. Looking down, I figured Sander was going to go with Tamara, and Aston would just blow me off.

"Hey, ladies, what's up?" Sander smiled.

"We were just riding the horse carousel," Tamara answered.

Sander laughed.

"What?" Tamara asked.

"Ain't you a little old for that?"

Ashton spread her arms and shrugged. "I like it."

I grinned at her.

She returned the smile. "Hi, Tyler."

I gawked and turned away.

Sander stood and lightly kissed Tamara's lips. I stood and Ashton approached me, still smiling. "Hey, Tyler, are you going to the dance tomorrow night?"

"I'll probably be there."

"You guys want to ride the Ferris wheel?" Tamara asked.

Sander turned to me.

"Let's do it!" I said.

I sat in the cart with Ashton, behind Sander and Tamara. The wheel started and when we reached the top, Ashton smiled, looking over the clustered grounds. How beautiful she was, with her long brown hair and light green eyes wide-open.

When the ride finished, we walked along the grounds for a while. Sander and Tamara held hands. I felt Ashton's fingers slide between mine. We headed towards the food stand and Sander talked about what idiots Daryl and Fenton were. Ashton smiled, staring at me. This felt as good as the first night we met.

"Sander, you never gave me a straight answer on whether you were going to the dance tomorrow night," said Tamara.

Sander shrugged. "I still don't know yet."

"We've been here every night so far," I said. "We might as well show."

Music blared so loudly from the speakers attached to the building that we had to raise our voices. I smiled at Sander, knowing if it were not for him, I would never have met Ashton.

Ashton and Tamara giggled as they stepped in the food line.

"Having fun tonight, Ty?" Sander asked.

I was having the time of my life, but just said, "Yes."

The girls came back, each with two Coca-Cola paper cups. Tamara handed Sander one and Ashton gave one to me.

"Thanks. You didn't have to buy me one. How much was it?"

She smiled. "Don't worry about it."

As we all sipped our drinks, Tamara looked at her watch. "Ashton, we'd better get going. Mom's going to pick us up soon."

"Okay!" She giggled.

"See you, Ashton. Thanks again for the drink," I said, bummed out that she was leaving.

"You're welcome. I'll see you tomorrow!" She waved as she walked away.

Sander turned to me. "I know you'll be here tomorrow."

"I plan on checking it out. You should come too."

Sander shrugged.

"Come on, what else are you going to do? And didn't we plan on coming here every night?"

"I guess we should find those two dickheads," Sander said.

# 18.

It was almost 6:00p.m. when Sander's mother informed me that he was with Daryl. I went over there and rang the doorbell three times and there was no answer. I doubted that they had left for the carnival already and wondered if they were at the clearing in the woods. I decided to just go home and watch for Daryl's car to return.

After waiting half an hour, I had my mother drive me to the church. "Thanks," I said, stepping out of the car. "If I don't get a ride home, you can pick me up at 10:30."

"How will I know if you got a ride?" she asked.

"I'll call you if I get a lift," I answered, swiftly. "If not, I'll be here at 10:30."

She sighed as I slammed the door. Checking the parking lot, Daryl's car was not there. But after thinking about Ashton and the dance all day, I really didn't care now.

At the carnival, I went to the food stand, and the guys weren't there. Continuing, I noticed bingo was not being played at the pavilion. Instead, a disc jockey had set up and lights were being attached to the ceiling.

Minutes later, I found Nate and Clyde standing together, laughing, eating popcorn.

Clyde smirked, noticing me. "Hey, Tyler."

"What's up?"

"Stopping to see us?" Nate crossed his arms and looked away. "What's wrong? Did Sandborn, Sunburn or whatever his name is, get tired of you?"

I just stared.

Clyde laughed. "Didn't know you hung with that crew. When did that start?"

My arms spread and I slightly shook. "We started talking again—"

"Right, I noticed that! And you haven't called me for a while. Guess I'm not as important as them."

"Are they nice to you?" asked Nate. "You used to want nothing to do with those guys and resented Sander for reporting you to the cops after you broke into his house." He turned away, still smirking.

My eyes bulged. I had never discussed that incident with Nate before. With clenched jaw, I turned and walked away.

"We're just messing with ya!" Nate yelled, laughing.

I thought it might've been best to avoid Nate and Clyde. I might say something that I'd later regret.

Going towards the concession stand, I wondered if my past was all that everybody remembered about me and if I could ever be known for anything else. I also wondered if Sander, Daryl and Fenton had purposefully left me out of their plans.

After purchasing a Coke, I sat on a bench and watched the DJ perform a sound check. I was a little bummed over the guys not showing up, but even more upset that they didn't tell me what they were doing. But after some of their recent actions, it was probably better if I wasn't with them.

I found Ashton, Tamara and a few other girls near the pavilion and I approached them.

Tamara smiled as I came closer. "Hi, Tyler!"

"Hey, Tamara." I turned to a smiling Ashton. "Hi, Ashton."

"So you didn't go with Sander?" Tamara asked.

"Where'd he go?"

Tamara's eyes widened. "Um, he said there was a party going on somewhere."

"Oh." I paused. "Guess I wasn't invited."

Ashton continued smiling. "Are you staying for the dance?"

"Yeah, I'll be. . ."

She turned away from me and started speaking with Melissa. I waited a few minutes while they talked and when she didn't turn around to let me finish what I was saying, I thought maybe she forgot I was even there. Walking away from the girls, rides and game booths, I sat in the grass near the school. It seemed nobody wanted anything to do with me. Since I blew off Nate and Clyde for the neighborhood gang, my closest friends didn't care to speak to me. Ashton would rather be with her girlfriends. I crossed my arms, placed them on my knees, lowered my head and closed my eyes.

As it grew darker, I walked back and saw ultraviolet lights shining in the pavilion. The music had not started, but young kids ran around hollering. Ashton, Tamara and Melissa were talking and laughing with the DJ while he prepared.

Minutes later, the music started. I walked towards the pavilion and watched Ashton kick one leg up at a time, bending her elbows in and out to the music. She saw me and motioned me to come over. Entering the dance floor, I attempted to mimic her moves.

The next song was, "Always Be My Baby." The other girls came in closer to Ashton and me as we laughed and danced. Ashton stared into my eyes and mouthed the lyrics, "boy don't you know you can't escape me, oh darling 'cause you'll always be my baby." I wiped perspiration from my forehead and smiled from ear to ear.

When a slow song started Ashton put her hands around my shoulders and I placed mine to her sides and we swayed to the music.

After dancing to several more songs, we went outside of the pavilion and talked.

"Thanks for coming, Tyler. Tamara was saying she didn't think many of the boys would show."

"I had fun tonight, Ashton. Thanks for dancing with me."

"Do you have a ride home?"

I looked at my watch and it was after 10:00. "Somebody's going to pick me up soon."

"Okay, because if you needed a ride, I'm sure Tamara's mom wouldn't mind dropping you off."

I wished I'd never told my mother to be at the church. "So how much longer are you going to be around?"

"Another couple of weeks."

"We should hang out before you leave."

"Definitely!" she nodded. "I'll give you my dad's number. That's where I'm staying, you know." She took out a pen and paper from her purse and removed the cap with her teeth then wrote her number.

Accepting the paper, I shoved it deep into my pocket.

Afterwards, the girls called Ashton over and she hugged me. She seemed so delicate in my arms and I could smell her hairspray. "Don't forget to call me."

"I won't." I watched her rejoin the group.

Trotting back to the parking lot, I only wished Sander could've been here to see me with Ashton.

# 19.

"Sander, sup!" I said loudly with vigor into the phone.

"Tyler! Hey, listen, I'm sorry 'bout yesterday—"

"It's okay, dude."

"I was at the baseball game."

I suddenly felt thrown off, because that wasn't what I'd heard. "Oh. I went to the dance last night and danced with Ashton."

"Cool! Are you going to see her again?"

"Yes."

Sander was silent.

"So, how was the game?"

"Phillies beat up on the Pirates, 5 to 1. Maybe you and Ashton can do something with me and Tamara sometime."

"We can do that. Who did you go to the game with?"

"Daryl had tickets, so I went with him, Fenton and another friend of theirs."

I was mute, having liked to have been asked, but was happier I went to the carnival. "So, what's up now? Want to shoot hoops? Ride the bikes?"

Sander yawned. "In a little while. I just got up."

"Oh, I'm sorry."

"No need to apologize. I'll see you later." He hung up.

---

Coasting on my bicycle down Gavy Lane, Sander strolled towards me.

I stopped. "Sup."

Sander twitched.

Getting off my bicycle, I walked beside him. Sander was just staring at the ground.

"Something wrong?" I asked.

Sander looked up and sighed. "No, nothin'." He paused "So, you hit it off with Ashton?"

"I hope so."

We continued to the playground. Once inside the fence, I got off my bicycle and walked with Sander to the center of the court.

"Good thing we don't have a ball," Sander said. "Or you'd get beat again."

He sat down in the middle of the court. I set the kickstand on my bicycle and plopped down beside him. "So the game sucked?"

Sander shrugged. "Might've been better if I wasn't with those guys."

I was baffled as to why Sander was so cordial with Daryl and Fenton when they were around but didn't seem to like them at other times. Then I thought maybe the guys had done something illegal while they were out—but I didn't want to know if they had.

"Tell me about the dance?"

"Danced with Ashton the whole time—fast and slow," I said, relieved he was changing the subject. "She's leaving at the end of summer. But we're supposed to get together before then."

"Right," nodded Sander. "You're supposed to go out with me and Tamara."

We talked a little longer then left the playground.

"Daryl and Fenton really piss me off," Sander said, walking alongside me as I slowly pedaled my bicycle.

"Oh, shit," I said. "What did they do now?"

"My dad's still pissed about them drinking in the backyard. I told him it was them," he paused, "and instead of talking to those two assholes, he likes to bitch at me. Anytime I go to do anything he says, 'I better not catch you drinking' or 'your friends better not come back here drinking.' Even when I came home last night he asked if I was drinking."

I wondered if all this was true.

"That's why I'd much rather hang out with you."

I turned, wide-eyed. "Thanks."

Sander didn't comment.

---

I called Ashton later that evening and we talked for nearly an hour on topics from the carnival to visiting her father. She giggled several times over my jokes and told me she'd talk to Tamara about all of us getting together. After hanging up, I was overjoyed.

# 20.

Near noon the next day Sander called, telling me to come outside. I found him atop his bicycle with a book-bag on his back. "Sup, Tyler!"

I sensed Sander's excitement.

"I was talking to Tamara and her and Ashton are going to the pool. Want to ride over and go swimming with them?"

"The pool? You mean at Chinook Park?"

"Right." He had a wide grin. "I was just talking to Tamara and her and Ashton are headed out there to swim and they invited not just me, but you too, to come out. Ashton will be in her bikini and I know you've been dying to see more of her."

I smiled. I wasn't interested in swimming and hadn't been swimming in a few years. But I did want to see Ashton in a bathing suit.

The park was over two miles away on Quarles Road and I imagined my parents might not think kindly of me riding there. "Have you ever rode your bike there?"

"Nope. But, hey, it's a nice day for riding. So grab a suit and towel and let's get going!"

I was always up for riding my bicycle and I wanted to see Ashton even more. The thought of riding that far was somewhat intimidating. But it would be worth it to see Ashton in her bikini. "All right. Give me a minute."

Going back into the house, I put on an old pair of jean shorts, because I didn't have swim trunks, stuffed a towel into a book-bag, strapped it around my back and came out. "Let's go," I said, mounting my bicycle.

We rode up Stanberry Hill Road to a gray brick church, made a right on Quarles Road and pedaled along the shoulder, passing many houses, a Co-Go's store and a small florist. Sander rode ahead of me and even with only seeing a few automobiles, I hoped nobody that knew my parents would see me, because they'd be sure to mention to them that I was riding my bicycle here, which I didn't think my parents would approve of.

Eventually we reached Micky's Pub and made a right onto Park Drive. Homes lined both sides of the street and it seemed much longer than coming through here in a car. Sander rode down into a cluster of trees and I followed him along a narrow path in the forest. "Why the hell are we coming down here?"

"We'll stash the bikes here," Sander replied, getting off his bicycle and hiding it between two trees.

I straddled my bicycle. "Do you think someone might steal them?"

"Well," Sander shrugged, "that's why we're hiding them here. We can't just leave them against the building. Somebody'd probably steal them then."

Stepping off my bicycle, I hid it next to Sander's and wondered if he ever thought of a chain.

Baseball and soccer fields were nearby as we came out of the woods and walked towards the pool. The park was larger than our neighborhood playground.

After paying five dollars, we went into the locker room where a shirtless teenager lounged behind the counter. A radio played heavy metal music and behind him, there were two posters of models in bikinis; to the right, shelves were filled with baskets. Sander changed into a bathing suit while I put on my old pair of shorts.

We found the girls resting on beach-towels, Tamara in a red bikini and Ashton in blue. Sander put on a pair of shades and stood over Tamara. "Looks like we found a couple hotties."

Tamara shielded her eyes and looked up, smiling. "I'm waiting for my boyfriend. But maybe he won't show up."

Sander and I laughed loudly.

Ashton sat up. "Did you guys get dropped off?"

I looked into her eyes, attempting not to stare at her body. "We rode our bikes."

"All the way from your place? Wow, I'm impressed."

"Hey, it's nothing," said Sander. "We do it all the time."

Tamara sighed. "No you don't!" She leaned over and whispered to Ashton. Sander took off his book-bag and shook out a towel next to Tamara and I put my towel in front of Ashton's.

Entering the pool, Sander swam underwater and the girls and I walked to the center, where Tamara straddled her legs around Sander's shoulders and he stood up. I looked at Ashton, who nodded and we did the same.

"Wow, it looks different from up here!" Ashton said as I held onto to her smooth thighs, balancing her.

The lifeguard blew his whistle and motioned for us to put the girls down.

"Knew that was going to happen," Sander said as Tamara fell back and splashed into the water.

We stood in the water, talking and laughing. A couple times, Sander dove underwater to feel up Tamara's leg. She would splash the water over his head and yell, "Stop." Sander came up for air, then quickly went completely under again, lifted her up by the knees and dropped her into the water, then did the same to Ashton.

"Hey, leave my lady alone!" I yelled. Smiling, I made a fist and pretended to punch Sander across the face. Sander quickly dropped into the water then came up and I faked another strike, to which Sander again fell backwards. As the girls giggled, I dove under, grabbed Ashton below her knees, lifted and dropped her in the water. The lifeguard stood and again blew the whistle, removed his sunglasses and stared at us.

Sander laughed, leaned back and backstroked away.

Ashton smiled at me and I stared into her eyes.

When the lifeguards blew the whistle for adult swim, we went back to our towels. Sander and Tamara rested on the same towel, pressed their bodies together and started kissing. Ashton moved her towel next to mine. "Have you been here much this summer?"

My body shook with elation. I had never been as close to an attractive girl in a bikini than I was on this day. "At the pool? Uh, no. Have you?"

She smiled. "I came out a couple times with Tamara."

I stared at her smooth legs and luscious breasts in the bikini top then hesitantly moved my hand over her thigh. She pulled away and I turned, embarrassed.

Sander and Tamara continued kissing and giggling as Ashton and I sat in awkward silence. "How much longer are you going to be at your dad's?" I asked.

"'Nother couple of weeks. 'Til school starts." She paused. "We should go see a movie, or, I don't know, go miniature golfing before I leave."

"That'd be cool," I said.

---

Tamara's mother picked up the girls, and Sander and I went into the woods to our bicycles. Sander was fully clothed and dried while I wore the damp shorts.

"See, the bikes are still here," smiled Sander. "And you thought they wouldn't be safe. You thought somebody'd steal them."

Pushing the bicycles out of the woods, we made fun of the lifeguard who blew the whistle at us and a large lady that rested in the grass. Riding was somewhat uncomfortable in my wet shorts, but it was well worth it to have seen Ashton.

We pedaled along the main road and a cool breeze hit us.

Sander rode onto Gavy Lane and looked over his shoulder at me. "What are you doing now?"

I shrugged my shoulders as we both panted.

"Want to shoot hoops? I ain't too tired."

I looked down, shaking my head, thinking I had a hard enough time beating Sander when I wasn't sweating and fatigued.

"Come on, Ty!" He smiled. "You ain't going to make me hang with dick Daryl and fuck Fenton, are you?"

I laughed. "Just let me change shorts first."

Entering the house, I saw Dad sitting in the recliner reading the paper.

"Hey, Tyler, where've you been?"

"Uh," I hesitated, "went swimming."

"Swimming? Where?"

Although I knew my father might not approve of where I bicycled to, I knew, from past mistakes, the truth was best. "Me and Sander rode our bikes to Chinook park."

He turned to me. "Did you ride on Quarles Road or find a back way?"

I bobbed my head. "Quarles Road, the whole way."

He turned back to the paper. "Be careful. That's a busy road."

"Will do," I said, glad a larger lecture didn't follow, then went to my room.


Late that night, I replayed in my head Ashton smiling and waving as she departed. I was consumed by thoughts of her while lying alone on the living room couch watching TV. I wasn't thinking about the inevitability of her leaving to be with her mother. I thought about the next time we would spend time together.

# 21.

I awoke with exhilaration on the couch in the morning, wanting to get out of the house and enjoy the day. I called Sander and said I was going to play basketball and told him to come up.

I bounced the ball up the hill, sometimes between my legs, sometimes behind my back, which didn't work so well, and I spun the ball on my finger.

A little more than thirty minutes later, Sander appeared at the court, his hair a mess. "You practiced up, buddy?"

We played with the same aggressiveness as we always did. With the score tied at four, I went to steal the ball from Sander and knocked it back. We both dove for the loose ball and our heads collided. I placed my hand on my sore skull and clenched my teeth, thinking Sander did that intentionally.

Then Sander laughed.

I got to my feet, growling and wondering what he was laughing at.

"You okay, buddy?" Sander asked.

I rubbed my head and sighed. "Yeah, I'm fine."

We continued the game and I won 10-9.

"Congratulations. You finally beat me," said Sander.

I placed my left hand to my head. "Now I can concentrate on my cracked skull."

Sander again chuckled, making a layup. "Sorry about that, Ty. Is your head really bothering you?"

"No, I'm okay," I answered, but still felt a pinch of pain.

We shot around for a while then left the court.

"Want to stop over my place?" Sander asked as we turned down Gavy Lane. Since Daryl and Fenton's drinking in the backyard, the three of us still stopped over the house regularly, and I wondered if Sander's parents were okay with that. "We can chill at the pit."

"Sure, why not."

We sat near the fireplace and discussed the upcoming football season before Sander asked, "So when are you and Ashton going out?"

"Hopefully soon."

"Yeah, you better hurry up and hit that. A girl like Ashton ain't going to wait long."

The comment reminded me that she was only going to be around for a short time. "Yeah, right." I bit my lip and looked away.

After several seconds of silence, Sander sighed and said, "Hope Daryl and Fenton don't stop over."

"You expecting them?"

He stared at Daryl's house. "No. But that don't mean nothing. You know those guys don't need an invitation to stop over and act like they own the place."

"Right."

Later that evening, I called Ashton and her father answered.

"Is Ashton there?"

"Who's this?" he asked, after a pause.

"Tyler."

"Tyler." It sounded like he snickered. "She's not here right now. I'll tell her you called."

"Thanks." I hung up and wondered why he laughed after finding out who was calling. Then I realized maybe her real boyfriend had called also. Leaning back on the couch, I closed my eyes.

Staying in that night, there were two calls and neither was Ashton. Sitting on the couch, I stared unsettlingly at the television as my hopes for a future with my dream girl decayed. Her father's chuckle, then her not returning my call, made me feel she didn't care to speak to me, and I desperately hoped that wasn't the case.

# 22.

The next morning I left the house, still bummed over Ashton not calling back. I hoped her dad just forgotten to mention my call. But deep down, I felt she didn't want to call me back. Perhaps all the talk about going to see a movie or miniature golfing was just an act.

Walking along the road behind Sander's backyard, Sander was sitting by the pit, smoking. "Sander!"

Raising his head slightly, he nodded, the cigarette hanging from his lips. I approached him, detecting his sour mood.

"Sup, Ty?"

"Sup." Sitting beside him, I wondered why he seemed down. "How are you doing?"

Staring ahead, he shrugged.

"Talk to Tamara?" I asked after seconds of silence.

"To hell with her."

"Why's that?"

"She's pissed at me because I wanted to chill with Daryl and Fenton over her last night. She said, 'Don't call me. Just go be with your asshole friends!'"

"Sander," I shook my head. "When you're around her or me, you talk about what assholes they are. But then when they're around you're all about hanging with them." I paused, looking at him. "What the fuck's up with that?"

Sander's head whipped towards me. He removed the cigarette, narrowed his eyes, and shook his head. "Bet you can't wait until school starts? You ain't got to go nowhere; just learn in your bed, shit in your own toilet, not have to deal with other kids. Nobody's going to judge you!"

I turned away from him, sighed and shook my head.

"You know, you really pissed me off breaking into my house, man! I didn't know those videogames meant so much to you. Why'd you do that? I bet those assholes Rick and Jester put you up to that! Do you still talk to those two fuckheads?"

My hands clenched as I turned away from him. If I looked at him, I knew we might fight. I started believing the only reason he invited me to the bonfires, played basketball with me and let me spend time with him and his friends was so he could find an opportunity to say that.

Standing, I walked away from him. Then he called my name. I turned, expecting an apology.

Sander shook his head. "I just ain't up for it."

I didn't really know what that meant and waited to hear if anything followed. When nothing else was said, I went home.

Minutes later, I pedaled quickly out of the garage, planning to ride over to Nate's condo, which wasn't far from where the carnival was held. Not wanting to think about Sander or Ashton anymore, I was set on spending time with one of my true friends.

The cool breeze hit me as I rode quickly along the street on the way to Nate's place.

Passing the bare schoolyard I thought of the good times had there recently. A little ways beyond the school, I rode by an antique store and a coffee shop then made a right up a slight hill into Chinook Arms. Coasting through the large alley between two large gray buildings to the visitors' parking lot, I left the bicycle there.

Going inside the second door from the road, I went up a flight of stairs and rang the doorbell on B-1. Nate answered after the second ring. "Tyler!" he smiled "What brings you out here?"

"I was riding my bike and, well, I ended up here."

"C'mon in. Looks like you need something to drink."

"Right" I said, wiping sweat from my brow.

Nate removed a bottle of water from the refrigerator and tossed it to me.

Sitting on the couch, I mentioned riding my bicycle, playing basketball and going to the swimming pool, but omitted Sander and Ashton. I grew bored quickly when Nate didn't say much and only nodded after everything I said.

"So, do you want to go biking?" I asked.

Nate shook his head. "Nah."

"Why not? You still have your bike, don't you?"

"Yeah, I got it." He paused. "But I haven't been riding in a long time. Last time I rode was probably with you."

I hadn't bicycled with Nate in almost a year. "So, what do you do for fun?"

"I like to play videogames and sometimes Clyde and I go out for ice cream."

Although I played videogames too, I thought that sounded extremely lame.

Sitting on the couch watching Drew Carey on The Price Is Right, I decided to make another attempt to try and get him out. "Do you want to go to the school and play basketball?"

"We can do that." He leaned forward. "It's a nice day, might as well get out."

"Still got your ball?"

He stood. "It's in my room."

Exiting the building, Nate carried his small green and white ball that he'd had for years. He held it in front of himself and I swiped it away and started dribbling.

As we got to the main road, I gave it back to him. "How's your summer been?"

"It's here. Guess I'm just thinking about college."

I looked at him with narrowed eyes, wondering why he'd be concerned about that now. He was a fifteen, like me, with three years of high school left.

"My grades have always been real good. I think I might be able to get into a great school. I'm sure I'll get a lot of scholarship offers."

"Got to keep them grades up for a few more years, buddy."

He nodded. "What about you? How's the homeschooling?"

I laughed. "I have some time until I have to worry about that."

We made a left along the narrow road across from the school. A grassy hill went down to the swing-sets and there was a slide next to the redbrick school.

"So, how's Sander?" he asked.

I wasn't expecting that question. "Sander? That dude, well I don't know about him."

"I don't talk to him and he certainly doesn't care to talk to me."

"Don't worry about that." I said. "You know, he's got these friends, our neighbors, Daryl and Fenton--"

"I know those guys too." He chuckled. "Real winners. They were in detention practically every day."

"Sander thinks very highly of them and that's his problem. If colleges gave scholarships to delinquent assholes, those guys would get a free ride into some great schools."

He snickered. "Aren't those guys your buddies too? You were with them at the carnival."

I sighed. "They gave me a ride there a couple times. But they really don't like me. Neither does Sander."

He didn't comment as we went down the blacktop driveway into the school area and to the court. I looked at the other end of the school, where the carnival was held and smiled noticing the pavilion where Ashton and I danced.

The basketball court's base was black with yellow markings and chain nets were attached to the hoops. A fence surrounded two tennis courts next to the basketball court. Nate looked at the ball as he dribbled while I continued staring at the empty spaces where the attractions were a short time ago.

"Think fast!" Nate said, passing the ball to me.

A few minutes later, we started the game, and Nate kept his back to me as he dribbled. He didn't shoot the ball or even seem like he was trying to drive to the hoop. When he finally did, I stole the ball and made a jump shot.

Nate barely played defense. When I drove to the basket, he would move out of the way as if he feared I would knock him down. It made it easy to score and I wished I was playing with Sander—because then it would be competitive. Our game didn't last very long and I ended up winning 10–2.

"You've gotten pretty good, Tyler. You must've been practicing."

I laughed, not wanting to say that I'd been playing with Sander.

I walked with Nate back to the condo, then got on my bicycle and left. I told him I'd call him. But I was in no hurry to do so. Pedaling out of the driveway, I thought maybe it wasn't Nate that had changed. I started accepting the fact that I'd drifted apart from the friends I'd know my entire life.

Turning into the empty school parking lot, I went along the grounds and again thought about all the attractions that were here. Spending time with Sander and Ashton were the best times I could remember having. Riding alongside the pavilion, I thought of

Ashton's cute face as we danced, and decided to just call her again.

———— ⚬ ————

Ashton's father answered after two rings and I rolled my eyes. "Is Ashton there?"

"Is this Tyler?"

"Yeah."

"Tyler, Ashton left this morning to go back to her mother's."

My eyes bulged and I almost asked if he was joking. She couldn't have left already. She and I made plans.

"Yeah, I guess they're having some big shindig over there for someone's birthday or something. She wanted to be there for that."

"Oh," I said blinking, breathing heavily as I felt tears forming.

"I don't know when she'll be back. But next time I talk to her, I'll mention you called. Or you can just call her on her cell."

"Thanks," I choked out before slowly hanging up the phone. The worst of what I believed could happen was happening. Ashton had left without as much as a goodbye. The few times with her, at the carnival, the dance in the pavilion and the day at the pool were over and would not happen again. Our date would never be. I knew I most likely would not see her again and fought back tears. Suddenly, whatever it was we had ended and every moment we shared together was for nothing.

I knew why she never gave me her cell number. Because she didn't want me calling her after she left her father's. I was just someone to occupy her time while she was here then she'd have nothing to do with me after she left.

Also, I knew my friendship with Sander was not as strong as I believed it was. He had told me what he wanted to say for a while now and I took his harsh comments about being homeschooled personal, knowing that's how they were meant to be.

Deep down, I knew that I didn't fit in with Sander, Daryl and Fenton anyway. Wiping water from my eyes, I wondered what the point was in making new friends. It seemed like they would just let you down.

---

I took my bicycle out of the garage and rode up Gavy Lane, pedaling harder and faster than I ever did before. At the top of the hill, I turned right on a dead-end street and rode between several trees and slightly uphill until I had to get off and push the bicycle up the steep hill over twigs and rocks. Making it to a path, I straddled the seat and started riding again.

Getting to a crest, I looked down a steep hill to where two large boulders stood. Staring down, I bit my lower lip. What if I just flew on my bike as fast as I could down this hill? Would I even make it to the bottom and crash into the rocks? Would I fall off the bike and break my leg? Maybe fly over the handlebars, land on my head and break my fucking neck? I could be lying on the ground, if not dead, too hurt to move and nobody would know where I was. Nobody's here to stop me. I could kill myself right now. Not that anybody would give a shit. I suppose my parents might care. But not Sander or Nate or Clyde. Daryl and Fenton would probably get a big laugh over it and smoke a joint to celebrate. Teresa could give a shit. She likes to come home, see friends, and when she's done with all that she'll spend time with her poor, little fuck of a brother. I stared down the slope, but knew I didn't have the nerve to go down it. Growling, I turned my bicycle and rode away.

# 23.

M y eyes lit up and I smiled when Sander's cell number appeared on the caller ID.

"Hello."

"Tyler, sup," said Sander. "Hey, you want to go out with me, Daryl and Fenton tonight?"

"Where're you headed? Back into the woods?"

"Nahh, Daryl wouldn't tell me what he had planned. Said it was a secret and to bring your bathing suit."

I felt excitement with a sense of adventure, happy over them asking me to be involved in something they had planned. But I also worried they could be setting me up. Still, the joy outweighed my suspicions. "Okay, when are we leaving?"

I heard Daryl's voice in the background then Sander's laugh.

"When are we leaving, Sander?" I repeated.

"Oh, about nine. Daryl's here now, but we're going to his place. Come over anytime."

"Sounds good."

Hanging up the phone, I had mixed emotions. Before the call, I thought they weren't my friends and decided to be done with them. Then Sander wanted to hang and asked me to bring a bathing suit. All this, hours after I was in the woods, contemplating harming myself. Maybe they planned on doing it for me. I thought it a good idea to bring my knife, just in case there was trouble.

---

Shortly after 8:oo, I got on Facebook. I was not registered and never cared to be before, but thought that maybe this was my best chance to communicate with Ashton, at least for now. I registered a password then started skimming through the set up pages. Of course, I didn't have a picture to upload, but that could wait. Then I searched for my first friend: Ashton Jensen. A picture of her standing next to presumably her boyfriend came up. He was tall and muscular with spiked red hair and I didn't need to see his picture to know I didn't like him. "Fuck you!" I stuck both middle fingers up at his picture then looked at the five other pictures of Ashton, three more with the same boy, one with three other girls and one with Tamara. I was thrilled to see her face again, even if it was on a computer screen. Then, I sent a message:

Hey, Ashton, it's Tyler. Miss hanging out with you! How are things at your mom's? Next time you're at your dad's, you, me, Sander and Tamara should all get together.

Leaning back, I carefully read over what I had typed and thought the 'miss hanging out with you' part sounded a little corny, but didn't delete it. I sent the message and hoped to get a response the next time I was online.

Minutes later, I shoved my knife into my pocket and wrapped my jean shorts in a blue beach towel. Not wanting my parents seeing me with it and asking questions I couldn't answer, I opened the bedroom window and tossed it into the yard then sighed with wonder over what the guys could've planned.

Walking into the twilight, I grabbed the towel and shorts then proceeded to Daryl's where Fenton and Sander were wearing swim trunks and t-shirts in the driveway. Fenton saw me, but didn't say anything, and Sander sat in the grass with his back towards me.

"Tyler!" Sander said, turning and noticing me.

"Hey, Sander." I approached him. "So what's going on?"

"Your guess is as good as mine. Daryl didn't say anything more to me."

"I know what he wants to do," Fenton intruded.

Daryl came out of the garage, chugging a beer then smashed the can and threw it back into the garage.

"We going to leave now, Daryl?" asked Sander.

Daryl belched and wiped his wrist across his mouth. "Not yet. Sun needs to go down completely."

I thought maybe I shouldn't have given into my curiosity as the three of them stood in their bathing suits.

"So what's up, Tyler?" asked Daryl. "I see you got your suit with you, now you need to put it on."

I thought about the knife in my pocket and how I didn't want the guys to see it. "I'll put it on when we get there, wherever we're going."

"Anybody up for a beer before we leave?" asked Daryl.

"No." Sander shook his head. "For all I know, we could be drinking where we're headed."

Daryl smiled. "Could be."

"I'll take one," said Fenton, walking into the garage with Daryl.

Sander lightly punched my shoulder. "What've you been up to, buddy?"

"Well, I found Ashton on Facebook and sent her a Friend request."

"Oh, you did?" Sander grinned, looking down.

"Yes." I detected sarcasm. "Her dad told me she went back to her mother's."

"She left without telling you?"

"Yeah."

Sander shook his head. "That bitch! I wouldn't even try to talk to her."

Daryl and Fenton came out.

"If she made plans with you, then didn't even tell you she was leaving, why should you search the world-wide-web for her ass?" asked Sander, shaking his head. "Dude, she led you on."

"What are you two pissing and moaning about?" asked Fenton, sipping his beer.

"Ashton skipped out of town without telling Tyler."

"That bitch!" yelled Fenton. "Well, that's why we called you over. We're going to go look for her and find out what's up with that!"

"Hey, what are you going to do?" Daryl said. "It was a summer fling and now it's over."

"Daryl's right," said Sander after seconds of silence. "If she said she was leaving so soon, you might not have gotten your hopes up to chill with her and have more fun with her like you did."

My eyes widened. I had never thought of it that way.

"You did have fun with her, right?"

"Yes."

"Not as much fun with her as I did," said Daryl.

Everybody laughed but me.

With Fenton riding shotgun, and Sander and me in the back, Daryl backed out of the driveway. After going up the road and making a right, I believed we were headed to Chinook Park.

My suspicions were confirmed when Daryl made another right heading along that way. The headlights lit the dark road with no streetlights as we past the homes and the pool came into view.

"Are we going swimming?" Sander asked.

"Yep!" answered Daryl.

I rapidly turned to Sander, thinking sneaking into the public pool was no different than when I broke into his house and was arrested. These guys held so much against me over that and now wanted to do something, that I felt, was very similar.

Daryl drove by the ball fields and the pool, made a right down a hill to the lower ball field and pulled off the road and into the woods and parked. "All right boys, let's go swimming!" Daryl hollered, shutting off the car. Exiting, he grabbed the towel he was sitting on.

Fenton laughed, stepping out, followed by Sander and me.

Daryl and Fenton cackled loudly, running up the hill.

"I don't know about this." I paused. "This is stupid."

Sander didn't comment and took off up the hill. I reluctantly followed.

Sander scaled the fence as Daryl and Fenton jumped into the water. "Are you coming?" Sander asked as he landed on the cement inside the fence.

I didn't answer. Sander removed his shoes and shirt then dove into the water. As they laughed, I thought that if I didn't join them, I'd be ridiculed. Exhaling loudly, I threw the shorts and towel over, grabbed hold of the chain-link fence and began climbing.

Leaping down, I twisted my ankle landing. "Fuck!" I expected the guys, splashing in the darkness, to ask what the problem was. But they didn't.

I removed my sweatpants and put on my jean shorts and heard the guys talking, laughing and splashing in the pool, not rushing me to get in and I pondered why I was even invited. I thought if I didn't go into the water, they might not even notice.

Plopping into the shallow water, it was cold.

"Tyler, where the hell are you?" Daryl shouted from across the pool.

My bones chilled and I shook. But it wasn't because of the water's temperature. It was completely dark and besides the splashing, the only noises were chirping crickets.

I quivered, moving along, hoping that the guys and I were the only living things in the water.

It reminded me of nights in juvie, when I didn't know if I was safe. Still, I swam out to meet them in the middle of the water.

Standing next to Daryl, he sporadically glanced outside the fence. "Yeah, Fenton and me did this a few times last year. You two will have to come here with your ladies! It'll be more fun than being here in the daylight."

"Hell with those bitches!" spouted Sander, his voice echoing. "Anytime you want a life of your own, away from them, they make a big deal out of it!"

Daryl and Fenton snickered and I thought about how when Sander and I were with Ashton and Tamara, Sander put down Daryl and Fenton and acted as if he wanted nothing to do with them. Since he's here with the boys, he was speaking negatively about Tamara. I thought Sander was the biggest phony.

"Yeah, I never told you guys, but a couple months ago, I came home and my mother had torn up my entire room," said Daryl. "Mattress was upside down, dresser moved and cloths all over the floor. She was looking for my weed. Guess the bitch ran out of hers and wanted to steal mine. Joke was on her, because I had it with me. But I beat her up—gave that bitch a black eye. And if my old man ever comes back, I'll kick his ass even worse."

Fenton laughed.

"He used to get real pissed whenever I'd smoke his," Daryl continued. "But if he ever gives me any shit again, I got a Louisville slugger ready for him."

I couldn't believe Daryl was saying this in front of me. Once I was released from juvie I was thrilled to be with my mom and dad again. And I didn't want to do anything to hurt them or make them think any less of me than I already had.

"Shut up, shut up!" Daryl suddenly blurted.

We all turned to see headlights coming into the park. As a car got closer, Daryl and Fenton plopped under and Sander and I followed.

It was pitch black under the water until the lights went over our heads.

I felt jitters and anger growing, wondering why a car was here. I feared somebody could have noticed us driving down and was coming to see what we were doing. Or maybe the police were called and we were all going to be arrested for trespassing.

We came up slightly to get air and saw the rear lights as the car drove away, then came up completely.

"Sorry, I forgot to mention, the cops drive through here at night. Like every hour," said Daryl, then he laughed. "And that's why I have to park the car in the woods."

I was shaking and panting.

"Listen to Tyler!" laughed Fenton. "He sounds like he just shit. Watch out for a log in the water!"

I sighed loudly.

"You all right, Tyler?" asked Sander.

I turned towards Sander as Daryl and Fenton started swimming. "I'm getting out of here." Swimming away, I didn't hear if he responded.

Getting out of the water, I continued to quake with rage, thinking of how I was arrested for entering Sander's house unlawfully and these guys scale the fence to enter the pool and act like it's no big deal. Drying off, I put my clothes back on, then sat in the grass and continuously looked over my shoulder, making sure a police car didn't come down for the next half-hour while the guys swam.

"You ain't up for swimming, Tyler?" asked Daryl, getting out and drying off.

I shook my head, wondering if Daryl even remembered the police car driving through.

I was the first one over the fence and the others followed.

"You guys up for doing this again some night?" asked Daryl.

Sander sighed. "Ahh, I don't know."

As we drove away, I just looked out the window while Daryl and Fenton spoke amongst themselves. Pulling into Daryl's driveway, Daryl invited us to come in, but Sander and I both declined.

Walking away, I heard Sander. "Hey, Tyler, wait up!"

I turned to face him.

"Hey, I'm sorry 'bout that."

My eyes widened, not expecting an apology.

"I didn't know what those two had planned. Didn't know they were going to sneak into the pool."

I said nothing.

"I know the cop driving around weirded you out—"

"Weirded me out?"

Sander's hands went up. "Okay, it pissed you off."

"What I don't get, Sander, is why you love being around those two. I mean, when you're with me and Tamara, you talk about how much you can't stand them. And with them, you talk shit on Tamara. You liked to bring up me hanging out and getting in trouble with Jester and Rick. Well, those two asshole friends of yours are just like the ones I used to hang with. And you know where the fuck that got me!" I was so angry that my hands shook, ready to throw a fist.

"You're right." He paused. "They are just as much of assholes."

I waited to hear if anything followed.

"Well, buddy, I'm going to head in now. Have a good night." He stuck his hand out. I hesitated before slapping it.

Going home, I was thinking I never should've taken up with the three. I believed their actions were worse than anything I ever did.

Upon entering the house, I felt relieved to be at home.

"Tyler!" Dad called.

"Hey, Dad."

"Where'd you go?"

Although the question wasn't unusual, nervousness set in. "Ah, hanging out with Sander."

"Teresa called just after you left."

"Oh, how is she? Everything okay?"

"Yes, she's fine. Just called to say hi and that she missed us."

"Sorry I didn't get a chance to talk to her." Going to my room, I thought about how upset my sister would be with me if she knew what I'd just done.

# 24.

Two days later, I sat at the computer. I still hadn't received a response from Ashton on Facebook and nobody had requested me as a Friend, either. I thought about sending Friend requests to relatives and other people I knew, but didn't feel like it. The only reason I joined Facebook was so I could stay in contact with Ashton and I was getting the strongest feeling that wasn't going to happen.

Not much later, as I sat on the sofa flipping through the latest issue of Hot Rod magazine, Sander came to the door. "Tyler, what are you up to?"

"Nothing," I answered, staring at him through the screen.

"Come on out and enjoy the sun, buddy! Summer ain't going to last forever."

I smiled, relieved over Sander's visit, and went outside. "What do you feel like doing?"

"I don't know—shoot hoops, go in the woods, whatever. As long as it's outside."

We headed towards Sander's house.

Sander sighed and shook his head "Those crazy bastards—you believe Fenton and Daryl, sneaking into the pool?"

"Well, we did it too."

"True. Let's not do anything that crazy again."

I was relieved to hear that.

As we walked along the road behind Sander's backyard, Daryl came between the houses towards us. "Hey!"

"Sup, Daryl?" said Sander.

"What are you two homos up to?"

I turned away, not wanting to see him.

"Trying to avoid you and your boyfriend Fenton," Sander responded.

Daryl did his annoying laugh then turned his head slightly. "Hey, Fenton got some beer. We're going to head into the woods. Do you guys want to go?"

"No, I ain't interested," I quickly answered.

Daryl's lip curled as he stared at Sander.

Sander looked at the ground, shaking his head. "I don't know."

"Oh, come on!" said Daryl. "You two ain't got to drink. I mean, I'd prefer it if you didn't. More for me and Fenton."

Sander turned to me. "Want to check it out?"

I didn't answer, wondering why Daryl wanted us to come so badly if they weren't going to share the alcohol.

"Come on, Tyler. We ain't going to sneak anywhere and have to hide from the cops. Just going to chill in the woods," said Daryl.

"Nah, you guys just go without me."

"Tyler, don't make me go alone with these two freaking nuts," Sander whispered to me.

I suddenly had a change of heart, thinking about how I had no friends and now Sander needed me. Maybe I was overreacting about everything. "Okay. I'll come."

Ten minutes later, I sat with Sander in the back seat while Fenton put a cooler in the trunk. After slamming the hood, he got in the passenger seat. Daryl started the car and backed up. "Yeah, thought Tyler was going to pussy out on us again," laughed Daryl.

Fenton and Sander both chuckled, which swept anger through me and I wondered what my friends were really up to.

# 25.

Daryl drove down the hill, passing the derelict grocery store towards the woods and pulled over next to two large trees. Fenton stepped out of the car as Daryl popped the trunk.

"See you guys down here," said Fenton, exiting and going back for the cooler.

After the trunk slammed, Daryl drove back up the road to park at the abandoned building.

"I thought you maybe were going to just park down there," said Sander.

"Nah, just dropping Fenton and the beer off."

Daryl parked alongside the building and we exited the car. Trotting down the hill, Daryl and Sander spoke amongst one another. Entering the trees and brush, Sander removed matches and a pack of cigarettes, put one in his mouth and lit it. I thought about when Sander said that smoking was no good and how Tamara didn't like it and he was going to quit.

They didn't acknowledge me, which was a common feeling I received from these guys as we went along the path and I wondered why they were so insistent I come.

Down the knoll at the clearing, Fenton sat on the cooler, attempting to start a fire with his lighter.

He looked over, seeing the cigarette clamped between Sander's lips. "Hey, where'd you get the smokes?"

"I bought a pack," Sander answered, removing the cigarette.

"Good," replied Fenton, striking a match. "You ain't going to be smoking mine for a change."

I didn't like being here with them while they did this. I had a feeling that something was going to happen.

———— ✂ ————

As dusk began settling in the woods, I sat with the guys in front of the meager fire, but looked away from them, feeling distant, as they laughed, smoking cigarettes and drinking beer. I didn't want to join in. I didn't even want to be with them and my irritation grew. Before, I didn't know where Sander was coming from. But now, it seemed clear. He was Daryl and Fenton's lapdog, content on following them around, wanting to be like them and couldn't think for himself. I despised all three of them.

Sander looked at me with a cigarette in his mouth, ashes smoldering off. "Why you so quiet? Still thinking of Ashton?"

I looked at him straight-faced, although I couldn't stand the sight of him. "No," I answered. "I'm over it."

"Don't worry Tyler," laughed Daryl, "another dumb bitch will come along."

My gaze was still locked on Sander. "How are things going with Tamara? Is she still pissed at you?"

Sander removed the cigarette and flicked off ashes. "I think we're going to be breaking up soon." He paused. "And I don't give a fuck."

Fenton and Daryl laughed loudly. Sander looked forward with a shit-eating grin that turned my stomach. I was angry. I saw in them everything that they used to hate about me. Not too long ago, they wanted nothing to do with me because I hung around guys that broke laws and were rebellious. It seemed they were chastising me for not being that way any longer. I thought about just leaving. Walking home and forgetting about them.

Suddenly, a familiar shrill sound echoed.

Daryl grabbed the cooler and we all stood. Hearing an engine running and tires smashing debris we fled up the path, leaving the meager fire burning.

# 26.

Daryl led the way and a quad came towards us from another angle, its lights flashing. We leaped off the path. Daryl dropped the cooler, ice and cans of beer cascading onto the ground, as we stumbled through jagged bushes.

Falling, I slightly twisted my ankle, got back up and continued to sprint, then stopped to rest against a tree. I panted, realizing the others were nowhere around and my heart thumped heavily, like it might burst out of my chest as the quads' engines rumbled nearby.

The woods seemed to grow darker and this place was unfamiliar. I feared the guys might've been caught.

Then another thought surfaced: Perhaps they had left me. Perspiration dampened my collar as I leaned against the tree, quaking.

An additional theory dawned. Maybe this was all a well thought up, calculated plan to get me into trouble. "Those motherfuckers," I mouthed, body shaking rapidly. The engines sounded even closer and I dashed away.

I thought the night was a blessing, making it harder for the pursuers to find me, but it also made it difficult to find the way out. Grinding my teeth and panting, I briskly jogged through the woods, searching for an outlet.

After a few minutes there was movement nearby. Unsure of what it was in the brush, I bolted, causing much noise tramping the debris.

"Tyler! Tyler!" Sander called. "Is that you?"

Stopping and turning, I growled then rushed at the dark figure I knew to be Sander and rammed my shoulder into his stomach, dropping him to the earth.

Sander howled and I rose and slammed my right fist to his jaw, then threw a left, which Sander blocked. I was then quickly and forcefully pulled off Sander, thrown to the ground so hard that the wind was knocked out of me.

Daryl got on top of me and punched me in the jaw.

"Kick his ass, Daryl!" yelled Fenton.

Daryl pressed his forearm against my throat and stared into my eyes, hot breath in my face. "Give me one reason I shouldn't?"

"Just get off of me, please," I struggled to say.

"We came back to find you and you start throwing fists!" Fenton yelled.

Daryl moved off me, but stood, with fists clenched ready to pounce again.

"Sorry. . .I'm sorry. . . I thought you guys left me."

Sander rose and walked towards me, huffing loudly.

I stood and faced him. "Sander, I'm sorry. I wish I could take that back."

Sander just stared at me as Fenton approached. "We were almost out of the woods, but we came back for you, asshole—"

"Forget about it, Fenton!" ordered Sander. "Let's just get out of here."

An engine suddenly revved and headlights tore towards us. Sander bolted and we followed.

I could see Sander ahead, delineated by the quad's lights. He ran through a garden of rocks and stumbled forward. I tried slowing down, but fell over Sander, landing on top of him.

"Don't move! Don't move!" the man on the quad yelled, stopping.

I rolled over and got onto my feet then noticed Sander's motionless body along the rocks. "Sander, Sander you okay?" I shook his shoulder, although I knew it might not be the right thing to do. The quad with a helmetless driver pulled up further and I noticed Daryl and Fenton were still nearby. The man shifted the quad into park and stood.

I gently shook Sander's shoulder again. "Sander!"

Sander moaned, and I sighed in relief.

"You boys are trespassing. What the hell were you doing up there?" the man asked.

Suddenly, Daryl ran towards him and swung a long, thick piece of wood like a baseball bat at the man's head and he went backwards as it connected.

I gasped as Daryl then busted the wood over his head and he screamed. Fenton stared at Daryl, wide-eyed as he kicked the man. The man shot up and connected a fist to Daryl's jaw.

I glanced down at Sander, who rolled over, grinding his teeth with tightly shut eyes. He didn't know that Daryl was fighting with the quad rider.

Turning back to Daryl, I saw lights coming towards us as Daryl raised the broken wood and was getting ready to jab the sharp end into the man. I rammed into Daryl's midsection and dropped him to the ground the way I did to Sander.

As another quad pulled up, Daryl punched me in the jaw and I fell back, clenching my mouth. Daryl got up and bolted away.

"Hey get back here! Get the fuck back here!" the man on the quad yelled. He got off of his quad and checked on the other quad rider. "Chuck, what the hell happened? Are you all right?" He helped him to his feet.

"I'm fine." He stood, breathing heavily and placed his hand to his head. "I thought that guy was going to kill me!"

The man turned to us. "What the hell were you guys doing?"

I didn't answer and Fenton only sighed. Sander groaned loudly and the man came over and knelt down to check on him. "What's your name, son?"

"Sander," he moaned. "My foot, I think it's broke!"

"Sander, I'm Bob. Let's get you out of the woods. Chuck, are you okay?"

Chuck walked towards me, still with his hand to his head. "What's that punk's name that attacked me?"

"Daryl Leness!" My whole body shook as I feared Chuck might punch me in retaliation for what Daryl had done.

"Chuck, that guy there stopped him from jabbing the wood into you," Bob said, helping Sander to his feet.

I felt relieved Bob told him that, though I didn't know if it made a difference to Chuck as he just stared from me to Fenton. "You kids were trespassing! And why'd that other asshole attack me? You'll have some answering to do to the police!"

Bob helped Sander onto the back of his quad. "We're going to need an ambulance for Sander. Chuck, are you able to ride your quad down to my place and keep an eye on these other two?"

"You bet," he nodded and his piercing eyes locked on Fenton, then me.

As Bob rode away, Fenton and I followed him to the house. Chuck rode his quad behind us, keeping a watchful eye. Going through the clearing, out of the woods down a hill, we found ourselves at Bruce Morolski's old house. I knew the days of hanging out with the neighborhood gang would once again be ending—in one way or another.

# 27.

B ack at the old Morolski house, an ambulance was backed into the driveway and two police cars were parked alongside the road. I stood near the ambulance watching Sander being placed inside then the doors closed. I glanced at Fenton, who stood at the driveway's edge. I knew he didn't want to speak to me and surely blamed me for the predicament. I certainly faulted him and Daryl.

The strobe lights of the patrol cars flashed, lighting up the dark street, but no sirens blared. Neighbors came out to see what was going on. One woman was even in her pink nightgown. I thought these people were very nosey and wanted to yell to them to "go back inside your damn house and mind your own business!" But I knew I was in enough trouble and didn't want to cause anymore problems.

My parents blue car arrived pulling behind Sander's father's truck. I sobbed, thinking this all too familiar. Even though I had tried not to return to my old ways, it was clear that I had. My parents would surely let me know how much of a disappointment I was and that they didn't know what to do with me.

I felt a hand tightly grip around my triceps. "Come with me, Tyler." Officer Sandrosik led me to where Fenton stood.

I stood beside the officer as we faced Fenton. Looking down, I waited to hear what the officer was going to say.

Officer Sandrosik sighed. "Were you boys aware that you were trespassing on private property?"

"No, sir," Fenton answered in a slightly mocking tone, shaking his head with eyes closed.

"Mr. Clifford informed me that he warned you boys not to come on his property before."

"I don't remember that," Fenton lied with a smirk.

Officer Sandrosik nodded, pressing his lips together. I thought he might have known Fenton was lying. "Don't go up there anymore," he said. "You're going to be let off with a warning. The Clifford family is not pressing charges against you. But you are not permitted to go back there again, and if you do, you won't be getting off this easy. Your buddy, Daryl, he's not getting off so lucky. Do either of you know where he might've took off to?"

Fenton turned away, shaking his head. "I ain't got a clue."

Office Sandrosik nodded. "Well, the whole force will be out looking for him. And you guys got lucky. Don't go up there anymore. Consider this your admonition!"

"Admonition, wow, big word," Fenton mumbled to himself.

I glanced at Officer Sandrosik. If he had heard Fenton, he didn't react. Then I thought of the cooler and beer that was lost in the woods and knew that the police must not have seized it. If they had, we probably wouldn't be getting off with just a "warning."

"How's Sander?" I asked Officer Sandrosik.

He looked at me out of the corner of his eye. "It appears he broke his ankle, but I'm not sure. I think he'll be fine." Office Sandrosik then went to talk with Sander's parents and mine.

I followed him, but glanced back at Fenton, who stood in the same place, appearing eager to leave. Then I noticed Bob Clifford and his wife, standing on the edge of the driveway. I was hesitant to approach them, but thought it a good idea to apologize.

Walking towards them, Bob's eyes locked on mine. "I'm sorry we went on your property."

No response.

"Thank you for calling the ambulance for my friend. We won't trespass again."

"I hope your friend is all right," said Bob. "And I'm sorry for chasing you guys on the quad." He paused. "Maybe I should've handled it differently."

As I pondered if I should ask how Chuck was doing, because I didn't see him around, I heard my name and whipped around at the sound of my father's voice. As my parents stood near the road and Sander's parents left, following the ambulance, I knew it was time to go. Both of my parents were looking down and Dad had his hands in his pockets. I remembered that being a trait of his when he was disappointed

Driving away, I sat in the back, waiting for a lecture. When nothing was said, I felt no ease. I figured they were building some sort of punishment for me and would wait until they decided on that before speaking about this.

"How's Sander?" I asked, breaking the silence.

"Don't know," Dad answered, keeping his eyes on the road.

His tone reassured me that they were disappointed in me.

As the car pulled into the garage, we exited and I thought I should say something. "I'm sorry about all of this. I didn't know we were on their property."

"You're just damn lucky, with your previous record, that you weren't punished a hell of a lot worse!" Dad snapped.

Mom embraced me so tightly I had trouble breathing. "I know you were just going along with your friends. You may not have known you were doing anything illegal."

I knew that wasn't entirely true and wondered if Mom realized it also.

It was even further evident by Dad's sarcastic laugh. "Yeah, Tyler, how's about staying clear of your friends for a while—especially Daryl. Better yet, you should just forget you ever knew him."

"Will do, Dad." I knew that was not a suggestion.

# Part Four:
# Unsettled Neighborhood
# Conflict

Justin Fleischman

# 28

O ver the next two days, I didn't leave the house much. I mostly worked out, doing pushups, sit-ups and chin-ups on a bar in the basement, and played the Xbox. It was the same things I had done when first released from juvenile detention. It didn't relieve the tension I felt over the neighborhood crew or anything in my life. And I didn't think it would. It was just a way to stay busy. My father told me that he read in the paper that Daryl was wanted for assault and battery and is still being searched for. I thought about the other crimes he had committed and thought he could've been wanted for other offenses.

I also started reading Mark Twain's The Adventures of Tom Sawyer, a book my mother had given me years ago that I never finished reading. But I had a new interest in it now, because I thought Tom Sawyer's relationship with Huckleberry Finn and his friends and Becky Thatcher was similar to my connection with the neighborhood group and Ashton. With all the trouble the boys got into in that story, very little of it was actually Tom's fault. At least that was my interpretation.

I didn't care if I ever saw Daryl or Fenton again, just like I didn't care if I ever saw Rick or Jester. I wanted to feel that way about Sander, but couldn't. A big part of me believed Sander was different, and that maybe we could remain friends. I wanted to tell him that, but thought the opportunity might not arise, at least not in the near future.

That evening, Dad called me into the living room and I thought I was sure to receive the lecture I knew was coming. I'd hear that I was "such a disappointment" and that I'd "never change." Staring at my parents, I waited.

"Sander was released from the hospital. He's home," said my father.

I sensed sympathy in his words and expression.

"And he's been asking about you."

I looked at Mom, then Dad, wondering what Sander had been asking.

"He told everyone none of what happened was your fault. He said that you didn't even want to go into the woods to smoke and drink." I believed that last part of that sentence were my father's words only. "I don't know if I believe that."

That cut me to the bone. I had fought the strong urges to smoke and drink and was appalled by Daryl and Fenton's actions. But with Dad's words, it felt like he believed I was just like those two.

"Anyway, Tyler," Mom intruded. "Sander wants to see you."

My eyes shifted to her. "Am I allowed, Mom?"

"Yes, go talk to him," said Dad, "because you're not going to be seeing him for quite a while."

I shook, knowing there was going to be a change in my life.

"We're going to have you stay with your Uncle Terry and Aunt Becky over in Enerton Valley," said Dad.

I was shocked. My father's brother was always kind to me, but I barely knew him. "Did all of you decide on this? When did you talk about this? What. . ." So many questions filled my mind and I did not know which one to ask next.

"We talked about doing this before," answered Dad, "when you were first released from juvie. We thought it might be better for you. Well, now we know it would be." He rubbed his hand down his goatee. "You'll be enrolled in Enerton Valley High School—starting your sophomore year. Getting away and starting over in a new public school, we believe would be best for you."

Over the last couple of weeks everything in my life had become such a rollercoaster ride and now, all of the sudden, I was moving. Walking away, I sighed, not quite believing that my parents were, all of the sudden, sending me away.

---

Exiting through the garage, I walked across the street, took a quick glance at Daryl's house, then cut through the Collinworths' backyard and went to the front door and knocked, feeling that would be more appropriate than going to the back. Sander's father answered. "Tyler," he said, straight-faced. "Sander's in the basement, go ahead down."

"Thank you." I removed my shoes, wanting to be completely respectful.

Opening the door and walking down the steps, I heard the TV blaring. Sander rested on the couch, foot in a cast. He shut off the TV and grinned.

"Well, I never invited anybody who punched me into my home before."

I stared at him, saying nothing.

"You'll probably be the last, too."

I remained mute, unsure of Sander's intentions.

"Well, did you hear the police are still looking for Daryl?"

I looked down. "Yes."

"Yeah, I guess that idiot went to his buddy Ron's house and Ron turned him in." He paused. "But Daryl took off before the police could get to him. So who knows where he could be." He paused. "I can't believe the cops can't track that idiot down. I don't know, maybe the police around here ain't that good."

I smirked.

"Anyway, I hope that guy's out of my life for good. I feel like such an idiot for ever wanting to be around that asshole. Look where it got me, laying here with a freaking broken ankle, got a girlfriend who hasn't called to see how I'm doing, but hell, I don't blame her. And my parents, well, they're always reminding me of how dumb I've been."

I looked down. "I'm getting lectured from my parents, too."

There was silence before Sander said, "I'm sorry about everything that happened, Tyler. I'm sorry I dragged you into all Daryl and Fenton's B.S. And I'm sorry I brought up Rick and Jester."

"I'm sorry too," I said. "But at least the Cliffords aren't pressing charges against us."

He groaned, turning his head. "I was really pissed at you for breaking into my house."

I closed my eyes and bit my lip. I couldn't believe he was going to bring this up again, especially after apologizing.

"When you first came home, I wanted nothing to do with you. Then, after a while, my parents would tell me they were talking to your parents. They had said that you were doing well." He stared into my eyes. "That was after my parents started going to church every Sunday. I'd sometimes go, when they made me, but really wasn't into it. One time a particular sermon was on 'forgiveness.' I'm pretty sure they thought about you. I did."

Not knowing where he was going with this, I glanced away.

"After a while, I believed they forgave you and wanted me to."

I looked at him and nodded.

"I'd see what Daryl and Fenton were doing and I thought that they were just like Rick and Jester."

I laughed, because I had told him that just the other day.

"And whenever those guys wanted me to hang with them and get involved in all of their crap, I never said 'no.' I should have." He paused, closing his eyes and taking a deep breath. "Anyway, I'm definitely done with those guys. My parents don't want me talking to them anyway. Well, I guess I couldn't talk to Daryl even if I wanted to." He smirked, shaking his head. "Here I am, fifteen years old and having my parents telling me who I can and can't be friends with. I know, pretty pathetic."

"They're right."

Sander nodded. "I know. I just wanted to let you know, I'm not angry with you and was hoping you weren't mad at me and I wanted to make sure that we were still cool."

"Yeah, we are." I paused. "I'm moving."

"What? You're moving? Are you joking?"

"My parents are sending me to stay with my aunt and uncle in Enerton Valley for a while."

"Enerton Valley?" He looked down. "We scrimmaged with the Enerton Valley Vultures in football last year. That's over an hour away."

I nodded, solemnly. "You're not the only fifteen-year-old whose parents make decisions for you."

Sander closed his eyes and nodded. "I'd still like to stay in touch. Give me a call when you get situated, my man."

I laughed. "Will do. And I won't be there forever. Thanks for hanging out with me, Sander. Despite getting caught up in all of Daryl and Fenton's B.S., we had some good times."

"Sure did, buddy."

This talk with Sander was the one thing I needed to have before going to Enerton Valley. Speaking with him and rehashing everything gave me closure.

"I would ask you to stick around for a while," said Sander. "But my parents, well, they allowed you to stop over, but they're being kind of. . ." he closed his eyes and shook his head.

"It's cool," I said, thinking of when my father told me to stay clear of the friends for a while. "I don't know how much longer I'll be around, but if I don't see you, I'll give you a call when I get to Enerton Valley."

Sander sat up and stuck his hand out and I shook it. "Take care, buddy."

Although I wouldn't say it, I always liked it when Sander called me 'buddy.' "You too." I hoped it wouldn't again be a couple of years until I hung out with Sander.

I went for a short walk up Gavey Lane before going home and thought about what had happened recently. But I wasn't thinking about the trouble we got in. I thought about the bonfires, riding the bicycles, going to the carnival every night, dancing with Ashton and going to the pool. I wouldn't forget these times and knew there probably wouldn't be more like them again.

# 29.

My parents were at work the next day. Still lying in bed about two hours after awakening, I stared at the ceiling fan circling at the slowest speed. I thought about what there would be in Enerton Valley and at Enerton Valley High School. I wondered if there would be any kids in the neighborhood my age and if the kids at the school would accept me. What would I tell people about why I was there? Other than the fact that I moved. Sighing, I rose from bed.

Going outside to get the mail, I found two letters resting on a cardboard box. Looking at the box, my name was written on it in big red letters. My eyes flashed and I dropped everything. Shaking, I looked around. No one was near, so I squatted and picked up the mail.

In the house, I stared at the box. It had no postage stamp or address on it, so someone other than the mail carrier had to have placed it there. I didn't want to open it. I knew its contents held something I didn't want to see. I also feared it could've been a bomb.

Reaching for the phone, I planned to call Mom at work. But then thought it would only worry her. I decided I'd just tell my parents about it later. I would show Sander first. He had been around a lot more places and knew more people than me, so I thought he might've known how to handle this.

Slowly moving to his front door with box in hand, I pounded twice on the door.

"Hold on," I heard Sander yell.

His eyes widened when he saw me and he was walking on a crutch. "Tyler, what's up?"

I showed him the box. "I found this in my mailbox."

He looked at it, then at me. "What do you think is in there?"

"I don't know. I don't even know who put it there."

Staring at me, he nodded. "You know who put it there."

"Well," I sighed. "Daryl's behind whatever's in this."

"C'mon in." He moved away and I entered the house.

"I didn't say anything to my parents, yet. Do you think it could be a bomb?"

"No." He shook his head. "Daryl ain't got the intelligence or even knows anybody who could put a bomb together."

I chuckled, even though there was nothing funny happening.

"Let's open this in the backyard. Can't be too careful," he said, staring at the box in my hands.

I walked before him down the stairs as he hobbled behind me on one leg and a crutch. Even though Sander assured me it wasn't, I still feared the box could contain a bomb. I was having second thoughts on whether or not I should've mentioned it to him. Maybe I should've just waited on my parents.

"Have you got something to open this with?" Sander asked in the backyard.

"Yes." I pulled out a pocket knife, but didn't hand it over. "I don't know if we should open it."

Sander sighed. "I know you're curious, Tyler. Otherwise you wouldn't have brought it over to show me with a knife."

I nodded. "You're right."

He leaned back and grinned. "It's up to you, dude. Either we open it now or wait for Mommy and Daddy."

I bit my lip. "Let's open it now."

# 30.

S ander slowly slid the knife through the tape and I was as close to the box as he was. If it contained a bomb, I didn't want Sander's face to burn and mine not to. Finishing the cut, nothing came from the box and I exhaled loudly. He put the flap over and we noticed two cat's heads. One head was white and the other brown.

Sander sighed, shaking his head. "We know what sick asshole did this."

"Daryl," I said gloomily.

Sander pulled out the note, looked at it then handed it to me. It read: IF YOU TELL ANYONE WHAT I DID, THESE CATS WILL BE YOU!

"You know of anything he did that I don't?" Sander asked.

I shook my head, wishing we wouldn't have opened the box. I should've shown my parents first. Because I believed they would discipline me for opening the box with Sander before they ever knew anything about it.

"I don't know, man. It's up to you," Sander said.

"What do you mean?"

"We can call the cops now, we can wait for your parents or we can hope he left this to try and scare you and then skipped town."

I started shaking and sweating. If I called the police, they'd just call my parents anyway. So I decided to call Mom.

Sander agreed to come back home with me. I stayed beside him as he slowly gimped across the street with the crutch. Inside, I offered him a drink, but he declined. He sat in the living room and I called Mom from the kitchen.

"What's up?" he asked after I finished the call and entered the living room.

"She's going to call my dad and one of them is coming home." After I said that, I felt like a wimp for calling my parents because I was having trouble with the bad kid in the neighborhood. I wondered if it appeared that way to Sander.

He looked away and nodded. "That's good."

Mom soon arrived and Dad was only a few minutes behind her. Sander stayed, even after I called the police and told them what I had found and who I thought was responsible.

Minutes later, I answered the front door after Office Grovel knocked once.

"Are you Tyler?" he asked.

"Yes." I moved out of the way. "Come in."

"I'm aware of the charges against Daryl," he said as my parents stayed behind me. "Can I see the package you allege he placed in your mailbox?"

Handing him the box, I thought since he said 'allege' that he didn't believe me.

He sighed, shaking his head as he looked inside the box at the decapitated cats' heads before pinching his pointer to his thumb removing the note.

"Tyler, did anybody handle this note besides you?"

"Just Sander and I. Oh, and of course Daryl."

He glanced at me. "You assume Daryl left this note with the cat's heads. There's no proof that it was him." Carrying the box, he headed outside.

My parents stood close behind Sander and me as Officer Grovel told us to be careful and notify the police immediately if anything else comes. Then he looked at Dad. "Mr. Dyson, the same goes for you. If you or your wife receive any strange mail or phone calls, let us know."

Dad nodded. "Yes, Officer."

After the policeman left, I walked Sander to his front door. Opening the door, he looked back at me.

"I'm really going to miss hanging out," I blurted, looking down.

"Hey," he lightly punched my shoulder. "Just give me a call sometime."

"I will."

We shook hands and as I turned and stepped away, the door closed.

Walking back, I thought about how I would be leaving in the next couple days. And with Daryl still out there, I felt I shouldn't. I feared he could come to the house searching for me. And with me being gone, my parents would be there alone to feel his wrath.

And I didn't know the limit to his hostility. I couldn't leave until the police found Daryl.

Entering the front door, I met my mother's eyes.

"Sander is a good friend to you."

I nodded, staring at her with eyes filled with unshed tears.

# 31.

S unlight had faded as I sat with Mom on the couch and Dad was in his recliner. A preseason football game between the Seattle Seahawks and the Cleveland Browns was at the end of the first quarter. As a commercial ran, we heard a bang outside the kitchen.

Dad stood. "What the hell was that?"

He stomped into the kitchen when it happened again. I followed. He turned the outside light on and went out the door.

"What the hell's your problem?" I heard him yell.

"Where's that fucker Tyler?"

I immediately recognized Daryl's voice and started shaking. My trepidation was overshadowed for my father's welfare. Because I recalled seeing Daryl trying to kill another man before and knew he might attempt it again. Without hesitation, I moved outside.

"There's that little pussy," Daryl said, seeing me and throwing another rock at the house. From the light, I could see his eyes were bloodshot and hair disheveled.

"Tyler, go back inside and call the police!" Dad said keeping his eyes on Daryl.

"Yeah, Tyler," Daryl smirked. "Better do what Daddy tells you to do or you'll get a smacking!"

"Tyler, get in here, now!" I heard Mom demand from the doorway. My eyes shifted to her and she was on the phone. I assumed with the police.

"Dad, you go inside. This is between Daryl and me!"

Unsurprisingly, Dad didn't listen to me. But I was shocked seeing him bolt to Daryl and ram his shoulder into him, knocking him to the ground.

I rushed over believing it possible Daryl could have a hidden weapon. After punching Daryl, Dad rolled him on his chest then placed his knees on his back and pulled up on his right arm like he was trying to rip it out of its socket. Daryl fought to escape.

"If you don't calm, I'll snap it. I'll snap your fucking arm off!" Dad yelled. My eyes widened and jaw twitched as my whole body shook. I had never seen Dad this angry.

Daryl quit fighting. Dad slowly released Daryl's arm then quickly hooked his other arm, pulled him up and placed his forearm around his throat. "Tyler, call the police."

"Mom already did. Be careful, Dad, he might have a gun or a knife!"

Dad applied pressure to his throat. "Do you have any weapons?"

"No," Daryl moaned with eyes closed and a little blood oozing from his lip.

Seconds later, sirens wailed and a police car pulled into our driveway flashing its strobe lights. The officer quickly exited the vehicle with pistol in hand and strode over. Placing his gun back in the holster, he took Daryl from Dad's clenches and threw him to the ground to frisk him and removed a knife from his sock. After placing Daryl in handcuffs and reading him his rights, he escorted him to the police car.

The policeman talked to my parents while making notes, but I didn't listen. I stared through the darkness at Daryl's house. Then I wondered if Sander knew what was going on. I wanted to run over to his place and tell him everything that happened. Then I'd challenge him to a game of basketball at the playground. Collapsing on the lawn, I remembered he had a broken ankle and it was too late to play even if he didn't.

Another police car came moments later and many of the neighbors came out to see what the ruckus was. Officer Grovel arrived and spoke with the first officer and Dad.

I noticed Sander's father walking over and he waved at me. Then I noticed Daryl's mother wearing a nightgown speaking with the officers. "I haven't been able to speak with my son in years. I didn't know where he was, I never knew where he was and I couldn't control him even if I did!" she hysterically cried.

I glanced at Daryl's silhouette in the police car. I was thrilled he got arrested. With me leaving for Enerton Valley soon, I wouldn't be worrying about him targeting my parents. Mom and Dad walked towards me as the officers returned to their cars and I stood.

"Well, that's over with," Dad said. I followed them back inside the house, where I expected Dad to say more about what happened. But he didn't.

That night, and everything leading up to it was not discussed between my parents and me again.

# 32.

Two days later, early in the morning, I had a duffel bag and suitcase packed and inside the back of the minivan. After finishing breakfast, I got on the Internet as my father phoned Uncle Terry.

Ashton had finally confirmed my Friend request. But I was disappointed to see that she still had the picture posted with her dorky-looking boyfriend.

After all I'd been through I hadn't been on the computer recently or thought much of Ashton. Her confirming my Friend request gave me hope that we could still communicate. But I didn't send her a message back right away, figuring there was a long drive ahead to think of what to write to her. Still, I printed out the picture of her and the boyfriend, and then got a pair of scissors and cut him away. Folding the picture, I put it deep into my pocket. Then logged off the Internet, snatched The Adventures of Tom Sawyer and went to see my parents.

Dad stared at me with solemn eyes as I entered the kitchen. I could tell this was something my parents didn't want to do. "You about ready to go, bud?"

I nodded.

Putting my hand up to block sunlight as I stepped outside, I immediately noticed it wasn't as cool as when

I first came outside about a half hour ago. I climbed inside the minivan as my father lifted the bicycle and strapped it onto the carrier attached to the back. Pulling out of the driveway, I looked back at the house, then at Daryl's and Sander's houses and wondered about the unknown that awaited me in Enerton Valley. I thought Ashton accepting my Friend request might be a sign of good things to come. Although I didn't know if I'd actually ever physically see her again. Opening the book, I started reading, figuring I could finish or at least come close to completing, The Adventures of Tom Sawyer before we got to Enerton Valley and I began my new adventure.

Justin Fleischman

www.ingramcontent.com/pod-product-compliance
Lightning Source LLC
Chambersburg PA
CBHW051649260626
47170CB00004B/1409